JUST A SIMPLE ERRAND
The Funny Detective – Volume 2

David Berardelli

JUST A SIMPLE ERRAND
The Funny Detective – Volume 2

FICTION4ALL

PART ONE

The Brat Vanishes

Chapter 1

The tall, gorgeous blonde every private eye wants to see waiting in front of his office door was not there when I arrived at ten that morning.

Even so, I didn't let it get me down. You have to learn to deal with disappointments in any profession. Most of the time, while you're waiting for the beautiful babe to sashay into your office, a short, fat man smelling of Old Spice and cigarettes will come in instead. Or a tall, broad-shouldered woman with a baritone voice and an abrupt, masculine manner--as in one of my last cases. It doesn't matter if the client is male or female--as long as they have money to spend.

I poured water, measured out the coffee, and turned on the coffeemaker. While it brewed, I sat behind my desk, swiveled my chair around, and watched Orange Avenue's morning rush-hour. Orlando has been my home since I was a kid. Despite the heat, the hurricanes, the traffic, and enough clueless tourists wandering around to cast your own zombie movie, I can't think of any other place I'd rather be. Like every other place, it displays its own unique personality. Summer mornings are all the same--bright, cloudless skies, eighty degrees at seven A.M., and ninety a couple of hours later. It seldom rains in the mornings. This event takes place in the afternoons, around lunchtime, and lasts about twenty minutes--unless, of course, a Cat-2 hurricane has decided to tear up the area.

This morning, Orange Avenue demonstrated nothing out of the norm. Across the street, the bank, tire shop, tune-up shop, and Smilin' Susie's, my favorite breakfast place, all bustled with demanding customers. However, the small parking lot facing our strip mall was nearly deserted. It was too early for the liquor store, tee shirt shop, and Chinese restaurant. And, of course, much too early for anyone needing the professional services of a crackerjack private eye.

The coffeemaker gurgled, telling me it was ready. I poured a cup and added one sugar cube. I'm very spartan about my coffee. I'm spartan in many other ways, too--except with women, of course, and Jack Daniel's, which I keep in my desk drawer for emergencies and medicinal purposes. I also use it for stress, contemplation, depression, euphoria, boredom, and other assorted situations that require a quick boost of energy, stimulation, confidence, and much-needed courage. I usually go through a couple of bottles a week.

I sat down and had my first sip of coffee. It hit the spot, so I had another. Then I went back to watching the busy parking lot fronting Smilin' Susie's. I wondered if I should rush across the street for one of their excellent sweet rolls. I'd had breakfast in my apartment, but Smilin' Susie's made sweet rolls to die for. Sometimes they were impossible to resist--even for no-nonsense, spartan guys like me.

The phone rang.

"Deacon Investigations." I decided to sound formal. I had no idea why. I *hate* formality. It makes me nauseous. I promised myself as a kid that I'd never be formal. But right now I was bored, and decided to try something new. "Professional," I said to the phone. "Discreet. No job too dangerous or too insignificant. Visa and MasterCard are accepted."

Then it dawned on me that a prospective client who hated formality might be on the other end of the line. Maybe one of those good ol' boys from St. Cloud who owned a ranch and wanted to hire me to find his old lady. If so, I'd probably just pissed away a sizeable chunk of cash. But it was too late to take it back, so I held my breath and hoped the caller would think they'd dialed the wrong number and hang up.

Silence.

"Anyone there?" I asked.

"I was wondering if I should say anything." It was Phil, my lovely ex-wife. "I wasn't sure I'd dialed the right number. I recognized your voice, but--"

"My answering machine confused you, obviously."

"That was a *machine*? Wow. It sounded so *real*. . ."

"It was me." I hated leading her on.

"But you just said--"

"I lied."

7

"But why the professional touch all of a sudden? Don't you usually just say, hey there?"

"Actually, I was trying out my phone etiquette."

"Your *what*?"

"Figure of speech."

"I see." A pause. "Are you feeling okay?"

"What makes you ask?"

"I haven't forgotten your frightening little episode just a few weeks ago."

"Which one?"

"You were hearing voices."

Phil was referring to the case I was working on when my dead buddy Mike first popped up in my life. Mike is the spirit of a young woman who died during one of my very first cases five years earlier. It wasn't my fault she'd died, but she'd still be alive if I'd been strong enough to pull her up before she fell from the balcony.

But she came back and appeared in the men's room of Kelsey's Bar just before I was hit on the back of the head. Naturally, I thought her appearance had something to do with the blow, and it scared me. And being the foolish idiot I've been most of my adult life, I told Phil about it. In hindsight, I don't know why I did something that stupid. Like most women, Phil has a terrific memory. Women by their very nature never forget the stuff you want them to forget. The remedy for this, of course, is not to tell them anything.

"Still there?" Apparently she thought I'd hung up.

I figured I'd try the casual approach again. It hadn't worked yet, but I was still hopeful. "Now I vaguely remember."

"Don't forget your head injury as well."

"Of course."

"How is it, by the way?"

"My head? Or the injury?"

"I'd have to say one is directly connected to the other."

"We're all fine and just peachy keen. I'm presently sitting in my luxurious office, watching my statuesque Swedish secretary sort some of my latest files." I don't have a secretary, but I decided to give her something to think about. Phil has done entirely too well since our divorce. She runs her own company, has a great office, great employees, a terrific Winter Park apartment, and a great shoe collection. Some women do nasty things to the men they divorce.

"You . . . have a *secretary*?"

By her tone, you would've thought I'd just told her someone had asked me to act as a sperm donor for some scientific experiment. "Stranger things have happened, you know."

"I'm sorry. It just struck me as . . . well, you've never mentioned her before."

"I didn't feel the need."

"I didn't think you could afford a secretary."

"How do you think my clients pay me?"

"I didn't mean it *that* way. . ."

"What *did* you mean?"

"I'm still trying to digest the Swede thing."

"What's wrong with a tall, statuesque Swedish babe?"

"They're usually very demanding, aren't they?"

"She enjoys many perks, working for me."

"Perks?"

"A luxurious office. Flex time. Four RAD days a week--as long as a generous amount of skin is displayed. Good bonuses as well as an excellent match with a 401K fund and--"

"I've obviously been misjudging you."

"How?"

"By thinking you can't afford all this."

"Some private eyes make good money."

"I didn't realize you were one of them."

Now she was being insulting. "Because I don't drive around in a Cadillac? Wear flashy clothes? Speak fluent French in those ritzy restaurants I'm not allowed in?"

"I didn't call to argue with you, Ralph."

"Really?"

"Don't sound so surprised. And I'm sorry if I've offended you in any way."

I hated when she suddenly pulled back and made me feel like a jerk. I could never understand how a woman could yank a guy right out of his good mood and get him totally riled without even breaking a sweat. "Well, if you must know, I can't afford a tall, statuesque Swede."

"I know."

That remark *really* pissed me off. Whenever she did that, I had to throw in a zinger. "I had one … once."

"A tall, statuesque Swede?"

10

"A secretary."

"What happened?"

"It didn't work out."

"I understand."

"What's *that* supposed to mean?"

"Well, knowing you as I do, I'd say you probably didn't hire her for the right reasons."

"What reasons are you talking about?"

"Could she type?"

Enough was enough. "Oh, hell, Phil. Why the call?"

"I wanted to find out what you're doing today."

"Really?" I couldn't help grinning.

"Really. And stop smirking."

That's another of the many irritating things about talking to a woman you once lived with for fifteen years--she can tell when you're smiling by the sound of your voice. "I'm just maintaining a pleasant expression."

"You're smirking. Don't deny it. But don't get *too* excited. Believe it or not, this is a business call."

"*Business* call?"

"I'd like to hire you."

I couldn't possibly have heard her right. It sounded like she'd said she wanted to hire me. "Huh?" was all I could manage to say.

"I'd like you to do a personal favor for me."

So much for the misunderstanding. I could tell by her tone that this had nothing to do with my professional expertise. Phil hated my profession. My being a private eye had been the source of our biggest arguments and the main reason for our divorce. She loathed my erratic hours, the sporadic

11

pay, and the countless trips she'd made to the Emergency Ward to see if I was still alive. She went ballistic when I came home with a black eye, split lip, or bruised ribs--and when I didn't show up for an anniversary or birthday.

Phil has always been one of those high-maintenance babes.

"This has nothing to do with my private snooping business, does it?"

"Not exactly."

"What, exactly?"

"One of my biggest clients has a daughter coming to Orlando this afternoon."

A client's daughter. Worse, a *rich* client's daughter. I didn't like the sound of this. I'd probably have to be polite and on my best behavior--two things that always made me queasy. I sincerely hoped I wasn't right. If I was, it was my duty to make this as unpleasant for Phil as possible. "That's nice, Phil. I'm glad some of your clients have chosen to bring others into this wonderful city--"

"I need someone . . . to pick her up . . . at the airport."

"Go on."

"That's it."

She couldn't be serious. "Let me get this straight. You want me to pick up your client's daughter at the airport?"

"Yes. . ."

"In other words, you'd like to me drive to the airport, find your client's daughter, and escort her to my car. You'd like me to do this instead of having a professional limo service--a company that does this

12

sort of thing as a business--tend to it. And you've shot down the cab idea because--"

"Ralph, please don't make this any more difficult than it is. I'm in a bind right now."

"Okay, say I do this for you. What do I do with her once I pick her up?"

"Take her to Lee Vista Center."

"And then?"

"You can drive back to your office and do whatever you do."

I stared out at the Orange Avenue traffic while my coffee grew cold. I didn't reply because everything I wanted to say would hurt her feelings. All I could think of was my cold coffee. I wanted to dump what was left of it and replace it with a couple of strong jolts of Jack's. I couldn't believe this. My ex-wife wanted me to provide taxi service for some spoiled rich kid.

"I know what you're thinking," Phil said.

My silence had obviously made her uncomfortable.

"I doubt it, but give it a shot, anyway."

"You're thinking of some subtle way of getting out of this so you won't hurt my feelings."

"You're half right."

"Which half?"

"I don't want to hurt your feelings."

"What about the subtlety part?"

"That's never been one of my stronger qualities."

"I'll pay you."

"That doesn't make this any easier."

"Are you working on something right now?"

13

"Not exactly. . ."

"Then what's the problem?"

"Baby, I ain't no chauffeur."

"I'm not asking you to be a chauffeur. I'm only asking you to--"

"Be a chauffeur."

"It'll probably take you less than an hour. I'll pay your hourly rate, plus gas--"

"Do you have any idea what my hourly rate is?"

"Reasonably. We did live together for fifteen years."

"What's my hourly rate, then?"

"I vaguely remember something around two-fifty a day, but that wouldn't apply here, would it?"

"That two-fifty goes for any sort of job, Phil. It pays for my time, the use of my car--"

"You'd charge me two hundred and fifty dollars for a simple errand?"

"I didn't say that. I only told you what my going rate is."

"Then what *will* you charge me?"

"Nothing."

"I can't ask you to take time out of your schedule and not recompense you for it."

"I said I'd do it for free. Don't piss me off and make me change my mind."

"But at least let me pay for your gas. . ."

"Don't worry about it."

"Ralph, you don't have to do this unless you really want to. I'll understand. It's just that this is happening at a very inconvenient time and no one else is available."

14

"Why can't the daughter take a cab? Or a limo?"

"Her mother asked me to handle this for them."

"What's wrong with her father?"

"He's in France right now."

"And when will he be back?"

"Tomorrow afternoon. His birthday is tomorrow. They haven't seen their daughter in nearly a year. She's been away at college in California and just graduated a few days ago. We all thought it would be great if we could arrange a surprise birthday party and have his daughter show up as the surprise guest."

"Is she gonna pop out of a cake?"

Phil didn't respond.

"Just thought I'd add a little levity to the moment."

"Do you *really* want to know why I'm asking you?"

"Sure. Let's go with that while I'm still on the line."

"Her mother was very insistent that we protect her."

"From what?"

"Strange people. Foreigners. Locals. Young, horny guys. Old perverts. Scammers. Ex-cons. Druggies. People living here under the Witness Protection Program."

"That more or less includes just about everyone, including me and you."

I heard her sigh. "Jackie's been very carefully brought up and sheltered all her life. We all know how dangerous Orlando can be. Especially you."

I didn't say anything.

"I'm asking you because I trust you more than anyone else."

That really did it. Now she was making me feel guilty. Phil was a champion at things like that. I always thought it was the Catholic in her.

"Well? Do you want to or not?"

"Sure. Why not?"

"I don't want this to be free. I'll pay you whatever you want to charge me."

I didn't want to argue any more. "We'll talk about that later, all right?"

"Ralph?"

"Yeah?"

"Thanks."

"No problem."

"I mean it."

"I know."

"You do?"

"Your voice always gets that throaty quality when you grovel."

"Ralph?"

"Yeah?"

"Quit being cute."

"You really want me to do that?"

"I know you won't."

"Why ask, then?"

"Force of habit."

Chapter 2

Orlando International has never been my favorite place.

People are nastier there than at supermarkets during Christmas, or church parking lots after Mass. The airport people dress neatly, talk like voice-generated computers, act like perfumed robots, and treat everyone with polite contempt. Since 9/11, the Security people handle everyone with the same finesse as a drunken college kid on a date with a half-naked stripper. I couldn't bring my gun into the terminal, and it made me nervous. Even a dynamite, resourceful private eye like me finds discomfort among hordes of irascible people.

I reached the terminal in plenty of time and found the gate without too much trouble. Orlando International isn't quite as confusing as most other airports I've been to. It's just a matter of finding the correct terminal, getting on the appropriate people-mover, and following the arrows.

Jack Frazier's daughter Jackie was twenty-one, five-two, and very slender. Phil said I'd recognize her by her long blond hair. Apparently she liked putting glitter in it and constantly experimented with hairstyles, but hated short hair and hadn't had it cut in years.

The flight had already arrived, and the passengers were filing through the doors when I walked in. I used my professional skills to evaluate each passenger at a glance as they shuffled past me. All the males were out, of course. So were middle-aged, heavyset, and black females, and those taller than five-feet-two. Several decided to make my life miserable by wearing heels, which forced me to do some quick calculating. A good private eye always expects the unexpected.

It took about twenty minutes for the plane to unload. I still hadn't seen anyone favoring Phil's description of Jackie Frazier and was about to pull out my cell when something caught my eye directly to my left. A short, slender girl with short blond hair engaged in energetic conversation with a trio of big, bearded, long-haired bikers covered in black leather and silver chains.

The girl looked like she'd just escaped the late sixties. She wore a sleeveless black tank top covered with psychedelic flowers painted in bright neon. She wore no bra. Her tight jeans were faded, and torn at each knee. Red flip-flops covered her feet. Her exposed navel displayed a pearl stud. Red glitter peppered her hair. A tiny diamond stud pierced her right eyebrow. Her ears were barely visible. At least eight studs formed a wavy line from the top, down to each tiny lobe, where large silver hoops dangled. She also wore necklaces, bracelets, and rings. Her bare arms were encircled with tattoos of barbed wire.

This girl couldn't possibly be Jackie Frazier. At least, I *hoped* she wasn't.

"Excuse me," I said pleasantly. The bikers turned toward me and shifted, forming a large hairy shield to hide their tiny friend. I straightened to make myself larger--which was pointless and stupid. Two of them were half a head taller than I

18

was. The third, an inch or two shorter than his comrades, obviously pumped enough iron to keep the exposed breasts of the woman tattooed on his left bicep round and full.

I focused on the girl through the maze of huge hairy arms. I said, "Jackie Frazier?"

She blinked. "That's me."

My heart sank. "I've been asked to pick you up and take you to your hotel."

"You're . . . my *chauffeur*?" She displayed the expression of someone who'd just been ordered to pick up a dried turd without gloves.

"I'm just a friend of your--"

"Aren't you supposed to be wearing a suit and holding a sign with my name on it?"

Apparently this was one of those chicks with a one-track mind. "If I was a *chauffeur*, you'd be right. But since I'm not a *chauffeur*--"

"You'd also be wearing a hat. And when you took it off, your hair would be combed. You're not wearing a hat. And your hair's messy and greasy-looking."

"My Italian ancestors thank you for the compliment. But since I'm not a *chauffeur*--"

"These guys want me to go with them and--"

"I'm sure they do, but this isn't exactly their lucky day. Your mother would like you to--"

"Get lost, Shorty," one of the bikers said.

"I'm not here to cause problems." My pleasant smile was quickly becoming much too heavy and awkward to maintain. "I'm just here to pick up Jackie. By the way, my name isn't Shorty."

"You're gonna find your ass in that trash can," the second biker said. He extended a naked arm and pointed to the large plastic white object near the fast-food mall down the hall. I caught a heavy reek of B.O.

"That one over there?" I asked.

He took a giant step toward me. "You got it."

"I'm pleased we're on the same page. But I must tell you, I'm not even *looking* for my ass. I happen to know exactly where it is."

"Well, you're gonna be looking for it pretty fucking soon," he growled. He'd also forgotten to brush and use mouthwash.

I sensed something was about to break. I sincerely hoped it wouldn't be one of my ribs, or any of my teeth. I couldn't see anything positive happening here. I hadn't even glimpsed a Security uniform floating around. I knew damned well that if I'd dropped a gum wrapper, someone big and bulky would've appeared like magic to escort me to the nearest trashcan. Phil was my only option. I had to give her a quick call and tell her this little bitch was apparently engaged in other pursuits and didn't appreciate my efforts to pull her away from her fantasy world.

The biker with the hygiene problem took another step in my direction. That put him about two feet away. "I don't see ya turning around and getting your ass outa here."

"That's probably because I can't do that while I'm standing right here." I knew that wasn't exactly the most sensible reply for this situation, but it was the first thing that came to my mind.

"Some kinda smartass, ain'tcha?"

"I've been told that once or twice before."

The other two chuckled. The first one said, "You gonna let him talk to ya like that, Smoke?"

"Wanna step outside, Short Shit?"

I was getting angry. There were three of them and each one was bigger, stronger, and probably twice as crazy as I was. But I had better things to do than exchange zingers with three angry bikers in a crowded airport terminal. "Actually, I'm quite content right here, but thanks for asking."

The other two roared laughter. Smoke turned red. His hands squeezed into huge white rocks. "You're askin' for it, Numb Nuts."

"You're going to get hurt, aren't you?" a woman's voice said softly beside me. It was Mike. She'd appeared just a couple of feet away, in her red tank top and tight jeans, looking just as hot as ever. I'd never been happier to see a dead girl before.

"Looks like it," I said.

"And I'm just the guy to give it to ya," Smoke said.

"Want some help?" Mike asked.

"The faster, the better."

"How 'bout right now?" Smoke asked. "I'll just pick your scrawny ass up and toss you down the escalator."

Mike had already disappeared.

"I have a better suggestion."

"Ya know, for a scrawny jerk, you sure have a giant set of 'nads."

The loudspeaker crackled. Mike's voice said, "Will the person with the tag KLR-seven-five

21

please move your motorcycle? You are parked in an unauthorized zone and will be towed immediately."

The biker facing me pulled out his black leather cowhide wallet. His friends immediately followed suit. The one with the bulging muscles tensed, forcing the tattooed breasts on his bicep to inflate another cup size. "Shit! That's *my* ride!"

The threesome quickly bulled their way into the slow-moving crowd.

I had to get Jackie Frazier out of here. It wouldn't take long before the bikers found out they'd been suckered and would be back in no time. But I wasn't about to make this pleasant for her. She'd made this simple task extremely unpleasant for me.

"Since we're alone now," I said, "let me repeat my purpose for coming here and breaking up your little leather orgy. I've been asked to--"

"I got it the first time," she said flatly. "I'm not an *idiot*, you know."

"Really?"

She gave me one of those tired glares Phil used whenever I did or said something stupid. "I graduated among the top ten in my class."

I wanted to ask if there were eleven in her class but decided to behave myself. "Wow. It isn't every day I come across such a gifted, reserved--"

"You're boring. And I'm so *totally* over watching you try to be clever."

"I can tell. You look tired. You've got bags under your eyes, and your makeup's all smudged and--"

"Like I just said, you're boring."

22

"Are you ready to go? Or do I have to call your mom and tell her you'd rather stay here?"

"Well, since those guys are obviously too stupid to know where to park, I guess I'm yours."

"Oh, goody. This must be my lucky day."

She pointed to the large tan leather suitcase sitting on the polished tile floor a few feet behind her. It appeared large enough to carry a window air conditioner and a couple of good-size floor fans as well.

"Is that a *suitcase*?"

"You don't miss a trick."

"I thought it might be one of the latest compact hybrids we keep getting from China."

"Not very funny, though."

"I'll work on it. C'mon."

She pointed to the suitcase again.

"Let me take a wild guess. You'd like me to carry that for you."

"You're my chauffeur, right?"

If she was so damned smart, why did her short-term memory appear to be switched off? "I told you, I ain't no chauffeur."

"Well, it's too heavy for *me* to carry."

"How'd you get it on the plane?"

She huffed. "A couple of the guys at school-- how else?"

"How'd you get it *off*?"

"A cool luggage guy brought it out for me. Then Zappa took it from there." She shrugged. "Picked it right up."

"*Frank* Zappa? I thought he was dead."

"One of the guys I was talking to when you broke us up. He didn't tell me his other name."

"How come you don't have a nifty wheel-carriage-thing to pull it?"

"Why should I have to buy something when there are guys all over the place willing to carry it for me?"

"Silly me. What was I thinking?"

"It's a long way to the parking lot, right? Unless your limo's right out through the doors."

"I didn't bring a limo."

She frowned. "What kind of chauffeur *are* you?"

"The kind who can't say no to a beautiful woman."

She sighed. "You're *way* too old for me."

"Don't get your panties in a twist, girlie. I was talking about my ex-wife." I grabbed the handle and yanked. It hardly budged. I had to use every muscle I could find to get it to clear the tile. I hoped it wouldn't snap a couple of my vertebrae, or pull my shoulder joint out of whack.

Phil owed me, big-time.

24

Chapter 3

I'd parked on the third level, about halfway down the aisle from the elevators.

At the time, I considered myself lucky to find a space so close. But now, since I was lugging around a leather-covered engine block, I wanted to kick myself in the ass.

"Is that as heavy as it looks?" Mike popped up, appearing beside me.

"What makes you say that?"

"Your face is all red and purple. And there are veins sticking out of your neck I've never seen before."

Twenty feet ahead of us, Jackie Frazier moved down the aisle, gyrating her hips the way girls did when they wanted to antagonize every guy in sight. She had a nice little figure, but she wasn't my type. I'd never gone for snotty, pampered, or arrogant-- not even when I was a stupid kid with raging hormones.

"I think it's inconsiderate of her to make you carry her stuff," Mike said. "Personally, I think she over-packed."

"Ya think?"

"I *never* packed that much when I was alive."

"Thanks. That helps."

"You ought to switch arms. It's much easier on your spine."

I wanted to drop the damned thing, grab Jackie Frazier by the back of the neck, drag her over to the concrete barrier, and toss her over the side. I forced myself to keep my cool. A top-notch private always stays in control--no matter what the odds. "I've decided to overlook this," I told Mike.

"Really? Why?"

"She's probably exhausted from her plane trip. Judging by her bloodshot eyes, pale complexion, and general bitchiness, she probably hasn't slept or eaten on the plane."

"I don't like her," Mike said.

"Neither do I. But since I'm doing this for Phil, I'll give her the benefit of the doubt."

"Sometimes you can be sweet."

"Actually, I'm a schmuck. Isn't that what you mean?"

"I was being nice."

I figured that once I got her away from the airport chaos, she'd come around. She might even act civil--at least, as civil as a pampered rich kid could act among us commoners. But when I finally reached the TransAm and set her suitcase down, I could tell instantly that I'd been unduly optimistic.

"What's *that*?" She'd spun around and gawked at my classic car as if it was some sort of disgusting swamp creature.

"Oh boy. . ." Mike shook her head.

"*This* is my limo?"

"Like I told you back there--"

"I know, I know. You ain't no chauffeur."

"You got it."

"But *this?* It's . . . a *wreck*."

"It's a classic."

"It's a wreck."

I wanted to hogtie her, tape her mouth shut, and toss her in the trunk. But that wouldn't go over too well. Besides, I hadn't brought any duct tape with me.

I tried a long shot. "Bring any duct tape in this suitcase?"

"Huh?"

"Duct tape. It's sticky, usually comes in a thick roll--"

"I know what duct tape is, thank you."

"You're welcome. So . . . did you bring any?"

She sighed. "Why would I bring duct tape on a trip?"

I wasn't in any mood for any sort of logic right now. But as I stared at her, I wanted to slap myself for not bringing some along. "Guess I'll have to do this the conventional way."

"You're weird."

"Thank you."

"I'm serious. I heard you talking to yourself back there."

"I didn't think you were paying attention."

She glared at the TransAm. "This classic . . . it's . . . *filthy*. Doesn't this town have car washes?"

"I'll have you know there aren't many of these left."

"They probably all fell apart right after the Civil War."

"They didn't even start making cars until forty years *after* the Civil War, brainiac."

She stared at me as if I'd just grown an extra head. "How about *that*? You're *not* as stupid as you look."

"Still want to overlook any of this?" Mike asked.

"Not so much."

Jackie Frazier scowled. "Huh?"

"Just talking to myself again."

"You do that a lot?"

"Whenever I get bored." I opened the trunk and heaved the ponderous suitcase one last time, taking great care to slide it in gently so it wouldn't crash through the floor of my trunk. Then I slammed the lid shut.

She was staring at me, a blank look on her face.

"Something on your mind?"

She shrugged. "Just wondering why you didn't bring a limo."

"I don't even own a limo."

"You could've *rented* one, moron."

"Why would I want to rent one moron? I just picked one up at the airport."

Mike covered her mouth.

"You're as funny as a heart attack," Jackie Frazier said flatly.

"I have my moments. By the way, what do you have in that suitcase?"

"My stuff--what else?"

"Sure you didn't accidentally toss in a body, or maybe half a side of beef, while you were packing?"

Jackie Frazier shook her head. "You're not funny. At *all*. . ."

***

It took me about ten minutes to get within a mile or so of Semoran Boulevard.

28

The heavy traffic moved quickly. Mike sat behind me, shaking her head. I wanted to shake my head, too. I'd much rather be tracking down a deadbeat dad than dealing with a pampered princess with no manners and one seriously bad attitude. Even deadbeats had more class than pampered princesses.

Jackie Frazier sat beside me, her hands resting on the big leather bag on her lap. She was careful not to touch the dash or lean against the door. I didn't know if that was part of her "careful upbringing," or if she just didn't want to touch my car. Every once in a while I caught her glancing at me and frowning.

"How come this wreck doesn't have air-conditioning?"

"It does."

"Then why don't you put it on?"

"I prefer the fresh air."

"It's broke, isn't it?"

"It needs a compressor."

"Can't you afford one?"

"I just haven't gotten around to taking it in. Too busy."

"This is *Florida*, Jack. It gets *hot* here."

"Really? I thought all that hot air was coming from you. And the name ain't Jack."

She reached into her handbag and pulled out a hand-rolled blunt. I couldn't believe she had the balls to do that right in front of me. And in my classic car, no less.

"Is that what I *think* it is?"

She stuck the weed between her lips and pulled a red Bic lighter out of her leather bag. "Probably."

"You're *not* gonna light that up."

"Huh?"

"I *said*--"

"Oh, get *over* it." She flicked the lighter and inched it closer to the blunt.

I pulled over and brought the big car to an abrupt stop in the grass. While the heavy traffic roared past, I groped for the cigarette. She pulled away. "Pervert! Stay *away* from me!" She mashed her right side against the door and pushed her arm out through the open window, keeping the joint at a safe distance.

"Don't hurt her," Mike said.

"It's really tempting." I snatched the lighter from her left hand.

"What the fuck do you think you're doing?"

"I prefer you don't light that up in my car."

"Well, *I* prefer that I *do*."

"You don't seem to understand."

"Understand what?"

"It's very simple. You're not gonna smoke that in my car."

"What *are* you? A cop?"

"A guy who doesn't want to get arrested."

"My lucky day."

"I don't know if you're aware of this, but this road is heavily traveled by cops."

"So?"

"Cops don't exactly approve of pot-smoking-- especially on their roads."

"Fuck 'em."

"I knew you'd understand."

"Cops are dumbasses. They only know something's going on if you tell them. Anyway, they're not gonna pay attention to what's going on in this wreck."

"You're not gonna hurt her, are you?" Mike asked.

"Only because I don't want to spend the next six months in jail."

"What are you going on about now?" Jackie asked.

"My conscience keeps telling me not to hurt you."

Her eyes filled the sockets. She must have seen the rage in my face. "You'd b-better listen to it."

"I am. And it's not an *it*, it's a *her*." Once again I wondered how long it would take me to get to the closest hardware store and buy enough duct tape to handle the job.

"Listen, Jack--or whatever your name is. Are we going to the hotel or what? It's okay if you won't let me smoke a joint in this wreck. I'll do it in my hotel room. Or are you gonna follow me in there and *really* gross me out?"

"How can I gross you out?"

She shrugged. "By following me into my hotel room."

"Silly me I should've thought of that."

"You . . . won't do that, will you?" She actually looked worried.

"Now why would I do something like that?"

"She is rather fetching--in an impish sort of way," Mike said.

I made no comment. I knew when Mike was egging me on.

Jackie Frazier squinted, watching me closely. "You're kidding, right?"

"Me?"

"You've been joking around since I met you at the airport."

"You have, you know," Mike said.

"Don't worry. I'm deadly serious now. Once I drop you off, you won't ever see me again."

"Promise?"

"I'd rather have a root canal."

***

Jackie stayed quiet since our last exchange-- which suited me just fine.

She was probably also miffed that I hadn't shown any interest in her. A pampered, self-centered young girl like her wasn't accustomed to rejection. It didn't matter one bit that I was too old for her, or that she didn't even like me. In her world, she'd just encountered a male who didn't immediately want to leap into bed with her. This was obviously new to her.

"So . . . you gonna tell me your name?" she said, shattering the wonderful silence.

"Why would you care? You don't even like me."

"I was pissed, okay? Don't tell me you never smoked weed."

"No, I won't tell you that."

"Then why won't you let me smoke?"

"I promised everyone I'd take you safely to the hotel. If we get pulled over or arrested, I'd be so embarrassed, I won't be able to show my face at Bingo."

"You're kidding, right?"

"About what?"

"*Bingo*?" Mike asked.

Jackie watched me for a little while--possibly waiting for a punch line. When I said nothing, she shifted in her seat. "You know my dad?"

"No."

"My mom?"

"Nope."

"So . . . how'd you get picked for this?"

"I've never been very lucky."

"I'm serious."

"So am I. One time, I bought ten Lotto tickets and didn't even get one number right."

She blinked. "Aren't there six numbers on a ticket?"

"Yeah. . ."

"Then you must've used the same numbers. How else could you have done that?"

"You tell me."

"That sucks. But it still doesn't tell me why you're the one who picked me up."

"My ex-wife knows your dad."

"Your *ex*-wife?"

"Ah. You're paying attention."

"You two . . . still *talk* to one another?"

"Still like one another, too."

"Why'd you split up?"

"That's kind of personal."

"How's she know my dad?"

"He's an associate."

"So . . . what's your name?"

"Deacon."

"Deacon what?"

"Just Deacon."

"No last name?"

"Tell her, Ralph."

"Why?"

"Why what?" Jackie asked.

"Why do you want to know?"

"You look like a Fred. Or George."

"People call me Deacon."

"That's your *first* name?"

"Ralph." I was getting tired of talking to her.

"So what's everyone call you? Ralph? Or Deak?"

"Deacon."

"Your friends, too?"

"I don't have any friends."

"Thanks a lot," Mike said.

That's all I needed right now--pissing off Mike. I shot her a glance. "You know what I mean."

"No I don't," Jackie said. "Everyone's got friends."

"I don't."

"Hey, you gotta have friends. What happens when you need help?"

"Help?"

"Say you get drunk, and the cops haul you in and you need to call someone."

"I'd rather stay in jail and catch up on my sleep."

"But … they've got all sorts of weirdos and creeps in jail. . ."

34

"News flash--they're walking the streets, too, girl."

"You're not afraid of being in the same cell with them?"

"I've been with quite a few women who've scared me as much any psycho, or pervert."

"That's cynical," Mike said.

"It's the truth."

"So jail's okay, then?" Jackie asked.

"Depends on what my biorhythm's doing at the time. Or if nothing's on TV."

She laughed. It wasn't pleasant-sounding, but more like a cackle. "You're funny--anyone ever tell you that?"

"You just told me back in the terminal that I wasn't."

"You weren't. Not then."

"But I am now?"

"Sorta. Anyone ever tell you that?"

"What? That sometimes I'm funny and sometimes I'm not?"

"Yeah."

"Once or twice."

"I'm serious, now. Don't you have any friends? Anyone you can depend on if you're ever in trouble?"

"I have this really hot guardian angel that pops up from time to time to bail me out of trouble whenever I get in over my head."

"I really wish you wouldn't tell people about me," Mike said.

Jackie huffed. "Hey, if you don't wanna talk, you don't wanna talk. It's no biggie, okay? I really don't care." She sat back and kept her face turned away for the rest of the trip.

I wanted to smile. Telling people the truth sure does give you back your privacy when you want it.

***

Using what strength reserves I had left, I lugged the girl's suitcase down the front lot of the Presidential Resort Hotel at Lee Vista Center, dragged it into the huge glittering lobby, and dropped it onto the lavish wine-red carpet. Then I sat on it and waited for my nerves to settle down while Jackie Frazier made her room arrangements at the desk.

"I sure hope you didn't break anything," Mike said, drifting over.

"You and me both." I wanted to shrug to loosen up my joints but was afraid to move.

A tall, slender young guy in a maroon porter's uniform passed, pushing one of those carts that transports luggage and garment bags. I wanted to kiss him when I saw the cart. I pulled myself up and hobbled over. "You wouldn't let me use that for a second, would you?"

"Sorry, sir." He paused only a moment. "I've got to take care of another room."

"Ten bucks?"

"I'm really sorry." Then he whisked away.

"A hundred bucks? I'll even wash your car every day for a week!"

He didn't miss a beat in his quest for the service elevators. I wanted to forget about kissing him and just shoot the bastard.

Jackie Frazier was halfway to the elevators when I turned back to the desk.

"Haven't you forgotten something?" I yelled after her.

She got in and pressed a button. "I'm in room two-twenty-two. Don't forget my suitcase." The door whined shut.

"She didn't even wait for you." Mike glared at the elevator doors.

I dragged the suitcase over. "I'm thinking of driving back to that hardware store."

"What good is duct tape now? You won't have to deal with her once you take the suitcase on up."

"I'm well past the duct tape thing. A chainsaw and deluxe pack of heavy-duty plastic baggies would make me feel just fine for the rest of the afternoon. I can take the suitcase up to her room, break her neck, then dismember her in the tub and slip the body parts into the baggies."

"How will you take out the baggies?"

"The suitcase." It was very simple. When you're all revved up, your mind works much more efficiently. "I'll empty it in the hotel room, transfer the baggies into it, take it out to the car and--"

The elevator doors whooshed open, jarring me out of my perverted fantasy.

"Damn."

"You were doing so well, too."

"A simple push over the balcony railing would be much quicker and a hundred times less aggravating."

"It's only the second floor," Mike said. "She'd probably survive the fall. How would you explain it to the police?"

"I was showing her the panoramic view when I sneezed and knocked her over. Anyway, I'm not afraid of the police. Explaining it to Phil would be my *biggest* worry." I gritted my teeth, picked up the suitcase, and went in. The doors eased shut.

"What would you like to do later?" Mike asked.

"For instance?"

"How about wining and dining me at one of the elegant restaurants downstairs? I'm getting hungry..."

"You're kidding, right?"

Mike laughed. Sometimes she was more annoying than I was.

The car eased to a stop, and the doors opened. I glared at the suitcase, then bent and grabbed it again. *One last time*, I promised myself. *Then I'll never have to touch it again.*

I lugged the damned thing down the hall and dropped it on the carpet right in front of Room 222. I wanted to turn around and get the hell out of there. Not seeing this through might get Phil in trouble with her client. I knocked on the door. Nothing.

"Let me have a look." Mike drifted through the door and disappeared.

I knocked again. Still nothing. I tried the door. Locked.

A short, thickset Hispanic maid shuffled by.

"Excuse me, ma'am. Can you open this door? I've misplaced my key."

She got out her ring of cardkeys and applied it to the door.

"Thank you."

She nodded and quickly moved away. As I turned the knob, Mike drifted back out into the hall. The grim expression on her beautiful face made me instantly nauseous.

"Are you about to tell me something I'm not going to like?"

"Open the door. You need to see it for yourself."

I pushed it open and went inside.

The hotel room was empty. Jackie Frazier was gone.

Chapter 4

My first reaction should have been immediate panic, but I really wanted to laugh, maybe even do a cartwheel.

But I knew that would be tacky. So, being the sophisticated and professional private eye that I was, I decided to let my brain slip into its usual state of cold intellectual resolve.

"This isn't a good thing, is it?" Mike asked.

"Not exactly."

"Then why are you grinning like that?"

"Am I?" She was right. In spite of my sophistication, I was grinning like an idiot.

"You know you are."

I had to remind myself of the severity of the situation. The girl's father was an associate of my ex-wife. A lavish surprise birthday party was involved, with important guests and relatives. Anyone who wasn't an idiot would notice the vacant seat between Mumsy and Daddy. "You know what we have to do, right?"

"Find her?"

"Unfortunately." I turned toward the hall. "Did you check this whole place? Under the beds?"

"Done."

"Behind the shower curtains?"

"Also done."

"Closets?"

She nodded.

"But you were only gone a few seconds. . ."

"When you can move through walls and furniture, you can check an entire floor in no time."

"Good point."

"You're not . . . angry, are you?"

"Why should I be?"

"I'm doing your work for you."

"After lugging that damned suitcase around, I forgive you."

"Thank you, but we still need to find her."

Being the eternal optimist, I realized I might be making this into something bigger than it was. The girl could be roaming around somewhere, looking for someone else to annoy. "She might've decided to check out one of the restaurants downstairs. She might be hungry. Maybe she actually hadn't eaten on the plane."

"That sounds good," Mike said.

My cell beeped. I fished it out of my pants pocket. The display said *Phil*. I sighed tiredly. "My ex." I took a few deep breaths. This calmed me somewhat. I was a crackerjack private eye. I could handle a simple call without screwing it up-- possibly even this one. I even put on my best smile, since Phil could obviously hear it. "Hi, there."

"No professional touch this time?"

"I decided on casual. I've always been my best at casual. I'm good at casual. I even look casual."

"Everything all right?"

It's not cool to lie--especially to someone you still have feelings for and who still has feelings for you. But I had no choice. "Why wouldn't it be?"

"You're babbling."

"When?"

41

"When you answered the phone."

"Because I was casual?"

"Because you were *babbling* about being casual."

"I babble a lot."

"I know. We used to live together. You only babble when something's wrong. Is something wrong?"

"No. Nothing's wrong. Everything's just fine. Just dandy."

"The girl's in good hands, right?"

"Of course."

Silence.

Terrific. Phil usually went silent when she began adding things up. Most of the time, Phil's way of thinking was a *good* thing. But not in *this* case.

"Why am I not getting a good feeling about this?" she asked.

"Because you don't trust me--in spite of what you say."

"It's not that at all. . ."

"What else could it be?"

"I'm nervous about all this."

"Why?"

"For one thing, Jack's our biggest client."

I sincerely hoped she didn't hear my gulp. "Your . . . biggest?"

"His accounts represent nearly forty percent of our yearly revenues."

"That would be big, all right."

"Jack's wife told me Jackie's been going through a rebellious stage. They think it's a college

42

thing. And apparently it was the first time she was ever away from home. I just hope it's nothing drastic--just the stuff we all went through at that age."

"You're probably right."

"She wasn't rebellious with you, was she?"

"How?"

"I don't know. She wasn't rude. Or obnoxious. *Was* she?"

"Define obnoxious."

"Well . . . how *you* get sometimes."

"You mean, like when my ex-wife sashayed into the living room one day in her sexiest black slip and told me she wanted a divorce?"

"Ralph, now is *not* the time for that. Besides, I don't *sashay*. I *walk*, just like everyone else."

"It sure looked like a sashay to me."

"Anyway, it's past history. So . . . did the girl give you a rough time? Ruth, Jackie's mom, said they haven't seen her since last Christmas."

"How was she acting then?"

"Ruth only said she was quiet and detached."

Quiet? Detached? The girl must've been on Quaaludes. "Really?"

"Was she quiet and detached with you?"

"Not exactly."

"So she didn't give *you* any problem, then?"

"Now why would she want to do something like that?"

"What was I thinking?"

"That's right. What *were* you thinking?"

More silence.

"You're sweating," Mike said.

43

"I know." I wiped my forehead.

"Know what, Ralph?"

"Just thinking out loud."

"Something's wrong, isn't it?"

"What makes you think something's wrong?"

"You picked her up, didn't you? At the airport? She was there, right?"

"She was exactly where she should've been."

"And she got in your car with you?"

"Sure did."

"Where are you now?"

"In her room."

"You went in the hotel together?"

"Just the two of us. We make a nice-looking couple. I know she's a little young for me, but--"

"And you made sure she got her room?"

"I watched her handle everything at the desk."

"Where is she now, Ralph?"

"Now?"

"Yes. Right now."

"I already told you, we're--"

"You told me you're in her hotel room. You didn't say where *she* was."

"Well, it's like this. Nothing's wrong, if *that's* what you're thinking. She . . . stepped out for a moment and--"

"Oh my God. You . . . *lost* her?"

"I didn't *lose* her, Phil. . ."

"Then where *is* she?"

"I . . . haven't exactly started looking yet--"

"Oh my God. This is *horrible*. This--"

"Calm down."

"How could you possibly--"

44

"I didn't lose her, Phil."

"Then where is she?"

"She might have gone to one of the restaurants. She probably didn't eat on the plane. I'll bet she's sitting at a table, chowing down on a double cheeseburger and fries."

"Go find her."

"I was about to do just that when you called."

"I mean *now*. Go find her *now*."

The urgency in her voice scared me. It wasn't like Phil to panic so easily. Usually it took something much more traumatic--like finding a gray hair. Or breaking off an acrylic nail.

"I'll find her."

"Call me right back when you do."

"I will."

"As *soon* as you find her."

"I will."

***

When we saw no sign of her in any of the restaurants in the hotel, I realized this whole thing was beginning to wreak.

Despite my growing anxiety, I had to proceed calmly and maintain my usual high degree of dogged professionalism. Bad enough Phil had already lost her cool. If she knew how I felt, she'd freak.

The Vistana Lounge sat sandwiched between the Sunset Restaurant and one of the super high-priced gift shops. The double glass doors of the bar were closed. The room was dark, but a few flickering candles lighting the tables and track lights highlighting the large U-shaped bar told me Jackie

Frazier wasn't among the patrons. To be doubly sure, Mike had slipped inside and came back out just ten seconds later. "She's not in there."

"The ladies' room?"

"Nope."

"Shit." I'd hoped the bar would have been the girl's first stop. Since she hadn't been twenty-one very long, the novelty hadn't yet worn off. If she was anything like my generation was at that age, she'd try the bar scene at her first opportunity. I'd taken her away from her newfound biker buddies, then forced her to ride in a thirty-five-year-old muscle car. To top it all off, I'd stopped her from smoking pot in my car. A pampered, self-indulgent bitch doesn't handle frustration very well. She'd definitely need something to help her cope. Since I hadn't smelled pot in her room, I assumed she'd picked alcohol because it was legal.

"Why'd she get on the elevator?" Once again, my first-class professional mind sprang into action, piecing together the scenario. "If she wanted a drink, she would've gone straight to the bar."

"Maybe she wanted to check out her room first."

"How long did it take us to get up here?"

"A minute or two."

"A pampered brat like her would spend more time checking things out. Everything would have to be perfect. She'd probably want a different room if she didn't like the towels over the Roman tub. Or the Roman tub itself. Or maybe the toilet was the wrong color."

"If she was as upset as you think, she'd want a drink more than she'd want to check out her room. They have room service here, you know."

"That's right. She could've picked up the phone and had a bottle brought up."

Mike shrugged. "When you were her age, did you enjoy drinking by yourself?"

"You're right. I'd better go in there and ask a couple of questions."

The tall, skinny barmaid watched me as I mounted the stool. She had large dark-brown eyes, a long, pinched nose, and collagen swelling her lower lip, providing that perpetual pout most women lust after nowadays. Her large-hooped silver earrings were partially concealed by her long black hair, which hung loose. She wore a low-cut red tank top and black dress slacks. Her black belt stayed fastened with a huge silver buckle that dug into her ribcage. It took me considerable time to determine that her breasts were probably cosmetically augmented. By the time I'd finished evaluating them, I returned my gaze to her face. She was giving me that look all women give when they notice you admiring their breasts. They usually won't say anything--unless, of course, they don't approve of your expression. I never understood why women spent a fortune on their looks, then freaked when guys ogled them.

"A Jack's on ice," I told her.

She went to fix my drink.

"They're fake," Mike said.

"I know."

When the waitress came back, she glanced at the stool next to mine, where Mike was sitting. "Who're you talking to, sweetie?"

"My dead buddy."

The barmaid winked. "Would he like a drink, too?"

"She's a she, and no, I don't think she wants one. Do you, Mike?"

"I wish I could."

"Mike?" The barmaid shrugged.

"It's a long story. Was there a young girl in here a few minutes ago?"

"Ya mean a *live* young girl?"

"Twenty-one, but she looks younger. She wears her streaked blond hair short. She's wearing a black tank top and faded jeans. She also wears glitter and studs--"

"You don't like glitter or studs?"

I shrugged. "Why?"

"The way you said it. You looked like you . . . well, you weren't wearing your happy face."

"Depends on the woman."

"Does your dead buddy wear glitter and studs?"

"Looks good in them, too."

"Thank you, Ralph. But cool it, okay? If she thinks you're crazy, she won't want to help."

"No problem."

The barmaid frowned. "This girl you're looking for . . . I take it you don't like her?"

I enjoyed it immensely when people paid attention. It didn't happen very often. "Not one bit."

"You're not . . . gonna *do* anything, are ya? Something stupid?"

"Define stupid."

"You're not . . . a stalker, are ya? Ya look a little old for her."

"Thank you."

"You're not a pervert, are ya?"

"Only sometimes."

"How about now?"

"Don't worry. She's still her parents' problem. I was supposed to pick her up at the airport and bring her here, but she seems to have disappeared."

She must have believed my story. "She was here. About ten minutes ago."

"Where is she now?"

"She didn't include me in her plans, baby."

"She left?"

"You got it."

I experienced a brief warm rush of relief. "I guess we were right all along. She had her drink, then decided to ride the elevator back up to her room."

"Ask her if she was alone," Mike said.

"I know what I'm doing, thank you."

The barmaid glanced at Mike's seat and frowned again.

"Was she alone?" I asked.

The barmaid chuckled. "Not hardly."

My relief quickly vanished. "Who'd she leave with?"

"Some guy."

I waited. She picked up a shot glass and began polishing it with her white cloth. I recognized the action. This one was bartenderese for "Money for answers, baby."

49

I slipped her a ten. She pocketed it quickly. "Fairly tall, lean guy. Maybe thirty. Nice-looking."

"Taller than me?"

"Stand up."

I did. She nodded. "A couple of inches."

"Anything else?"

"He had dirty blond hair."

"Thanks." I finished my drink, put down another ten, and got up.

The barmaid said, "I just thought of something else. *Two* things."

"What's that?"

"I don't know if it's important. . ."

Whenever someone says that, you can be damned sure it's important. "Go on, give her a shot."

"Guy drives a red Corvette. I saw him pull in earlier, when I came in to work."

"Convertible?"

"Uh-huh."

Some people just don't like using their brain cells. Others don't seem to know how. Both types aggravated me half to death. "How about the other thing?"

"He's got a tatt on his neck."

"Where?"

"Left side."

"What is it?"

"It says 'Manta.'"

"Thanks." I turned to leave.

"Think it's important?"

I gave her a pleasant smile.

Sometimes a pleasant smile accomplishes much more than just coming right out and asking a person if she was ever dropped on her head as a child.

Chapter 5

Mike and I rode the elevator back up. Another wandering maid passed as the doors opened.

"Want me to ask her to open the room?" Mike asked.

"You sure are in rare form today." That's all we needed--sending the hotel staff into a panic. I flagged down the maid and asked her to open the door to Room 222. Hopefully, the girl would be inside with the guy she'd picked up, doing the horizontal mambo--or lying in the big double bed, sharing a joint. Then I could finally leave this place, call Phil, tell her the good news, then get back to my office and wait for that stacked blonde again.

Luck just wasn't cooperating. The suite was still empty.

Before we left, I glanced at the suitcase, which remained where I'd left it in the center of the foyer.

"You're not gonna toss it over the balcony, are you?" Mike asked.

"That would require me to pick it up again." I set it down on its side and checked to see if it was locked. It wasn't, so I opened it.

Apparently, the girl liked working out to maintain her svelte figure. Besides her top-of-the-line clothing, sheer underwear, and several large boxes of French lubricated condoms, two-, three-, five-, eight-, ten-, and twelve-pound pink dumbbells sat on top of a large red bath towel. I couldn't believe it. I'd lugged eighty pounds of added dead weight all the way from the terminal. No wonder I felt as if I'd been slammed by a passing SUV.

"Something about this doesn't make sense." The hairs on the back of my neck bristled--as they usually did when my highly-trained brain picked up something but wouldn't tell me exactly what it was.

"Is it the fact that she works out? Or is it something else?"

It was something else--although I just couldn't put it together right now. "I wish I knew."

We left the room and got back in the elevator. My cell buzzed as soon as we got out on the ground floor.

"What's happening?" Phil asked.

"I really can't talk now." We crossed the lobby fairly quickly. I needed to find the guy with the red Vette. I snuck a quick glance at the glass doors facing the entrance. I didn't expect to see it, but stranger things have happened.

"Ralph?"

"I'll call you right back." I pocketed the cell and went over to the desk. The desk clerk--tall and skinny, with a protruding Adam's apple and a pronounced cleft in his square chin--had just hung up the phone and attempted to show me his back. "Excuse me," I said quickly.

"Yes?" The arrogance showed clearly in the instant frown. The large circles of sweat darkening my polo shirt, made from lugging around the girl's portable home gym, obviously did not belong in such a ritzy atmosphere.

"Is there a young guy staying here? About thirty? Six feet tall? Sandy hair? He also has a--"

53

"Are you a guest, sir?"

"No."

"Then I'm not at liberty to--"

"Listen. I need to find out--"

"If you're not a guest, I cannot help you. . ."

"Would it speed things along if I showed you some ID?" I groped for my wallet.

"This is a *hotel*, sir. We maintain a high standard of privacy for our *guests,* and do not permit those who are *not* guests to question us about them."

"I think you need to be a little more intimidating," Mike said.

"Obviously."

"I'm pleased you understand, sir."

I hated lowering my standards, but with some people you just can't start up a quick friendship without tossing in a threat or two. "Have you heard of a man named Neil Haversack?"

The clerk sighed. "Sir, I haven't the time to--"

"He's a friend of mine. He's not staying here because he's working at the moment. He lives in Orlando. He's a cop. A Police Sergeant."

"Sir . . . what does *any* of this have to do--"

"The man I'm looking for could be involved in a kidnapping. He might have kidnapped someone who's a guest of this hotel. This guest is female. If I call my friend at OPD and tell him my suspicions about what might be going on in this hotel--"

"One moment, please." The clerk typed busily, then pulled a sheet of paper from the printer on his

54

left and handed it to me. "The man's name is Smith, sir. Alan Smith."

Terrific. There were probably three pages of Alan Smith's in the phone book. The sheet provided credit card information--which would help if the card wasn't stolen. The card was American Express under the name A. P. Smith. Nothing else. "Got anything on the car?"

"I'm sorry, sir."

"What kind of place *is* this? If *I* were checking in, you'd want my name, address, social, blood type, tag number, sexual preferences, political affiliations, next of kin--"

"I'm afraid this person must have checked in when I was taking my break, sir. Otherwise, I would have insisted on more--"

"Gotcha." Mike and I made a mad dash for the front doors. Once outside, we scanned the parking lot. The red Vette was nowhere in sight.

***

I called Neil Haversack on our way back out front to the parking lot.

When his recording came on, I left my message, got in the TransAm, and rolled down the windows.

"Hot, isn't it?" Mike said, appearing beside me on the seat.

I wondered if she was teasing me again. Sometimes you just couldn't tell. "You can feel the heat?"

"I'm just going by the sweat rolling down your cheeks."

"Yeah, you could say it's pretty toasty right now." I really had to bite the bullet and take the car in. The quote for the damned compressor was ridiculous, but mechanics have you by the short curlies. You can't go very long without a/c in Florida. And since developers have chopped down nearly every available tree in the state, finding shade is a losing battle.

"What's our next move?" she asked. "Finding the guy who left the bar with the girl? The A. P. Smith guy?"

"If that's his name." I didn't know where else to start. I couldn't ask Phil to question the girl's mother. Phil wasn't a private eye and wouldn't ask the right questions. And the mother would suspect something had happened. Hopefully, Neil might have something for me.

My cell buzzed. "Please don't hang up on me again," Phil said. "If I didn't know you, I'd suspect you were trying to avoid me."

"Sorry about that. I had to move fast and didn't want to waste any time."

"Talking to me is wasting time?"

Explaining myself to my ex-wife, who'd been analyzing everything I ever said since we'd first met nearly twenty years ago, always becomes frustrating. But since she was facing a crisis, she was more amenable than usual. "I didn't have anything to tell you and wanted to find someone who might know something."

"Did you?"

"Did I what?"

"Find someone."

56

"Yes."

"Who?"

"Two people, actually. I went to the bar and talked to the barmaid."

"Why her?"

"I always target whoever's tending the bar. They seem to know everything."

"I don't understand."

"You don't go to bars."

"How can you say that? I've just been to--"

"You don't go to *bars*, Phil. You go to dining rooms, banquets, and ballrooms. You stand in little groups and discuss Picasso and Ayn Rand and the Ottoman Empire, and every ten seconds or so, a little guy carrying a silver tray comes by with champagne, and those funny crackers smeared with fish eggs that go for a hundred bucks an ounce--"

"The Ottoman Empire?"

"I'm trying to make a point."

"Ralph, what does all that have to do with anything?"

"I'm trying to tell you why I question bar people."

"Oh. It sounds like you've decided once again to find fault with my lifestyle."

"I also talked to the front desk clerk. I figured that if the barmaid didn't see anything, the desk clerk did."

"So . . . was Jackie in the bar?"

"Yeah."

"Oh, dear."

"Don't go temperance on me now. She's of legal age."

"I'm just visualizing all sorts of things, and none of them are good."

"Don't lose it quite yet. I found out a couple of things that *might* help."

"What did you find out?"

"Someone might have left the bar with the girl."

"Any idea where they went?"

"Not yet."

"When will you know?"

"I know one thing so far. She's not in the hotel."

"How could you possibly know *that*?"

"There's a guy involved. He's the one who left with her."

Silence. She was probably contemplating whether she should bite off her acrylic nails or scream. As a precaution, I held the phone away from my ear. She'd decide pretty quickly that her nails had cost her a fortune. A scream didn't cost anything. But I heard only silence.

"Still there?" I asked.

"I *knew* this was bad."

"Like I said, don't lose it. That's all I know for now."

"But she's not where she's supposed to be. Isn't that bad enough?"

"That doesn't necessarily mean she's in any trouble."

"How do you know? Because she left with this man?"

"She left willingly."

"Try telling that to her mother."

"Just give me a little time, okay? I'll find her."

"The birthday party is tomorrow, you know."

"I know."

"Ralph, I appreciate your determination, but let's face it--this is a large, busy place."

"It's my fault I lost her. I don't intend to let that slide."

"You always were very stubborn."

"We're talking about my reputation now."

"How so?"

"If anyone finds out I can't handle a simple babysitting job, I'll never work in this town again."

***

Neil Haversack returned my call as soon as I finished talking to Phil. "What's going on? Your message said urgent."

"I might be in trouble."

"*That's* no surprise. Who is it this time? Raguzzo? I thought you two were bosom buds."

"I don't know about *that*, but we do have a sort of truce going on."

"That's what I call progress. It's kind of sweet, too. Gets me right here."

"I can't see what you're doing."

"Use your imagination."

"*That's* a low blow. Even for a cop."

"You've got a dirty mind, Deacon."

"I'm half-Italian."

"I'd think the Irish part would be just as bad. So who'd you piss off this time?"

"My ex-wife."

A pause. "I thought ex-wives were finished being pissed off. Except when there are kids and child support to contend with."

"In our case, things are slightly more complicated."

"I think I'd be less confused if you just told me what's going on. I'm what you'd call rushed right now."

"One of her clients is having a birthday party tomorrow and his wife arranged to have their daughter here as a surprise. She's a college grad and a real handful."

"This still doesn't tell me how you pissed off your ex."

"I was supposed to pick up the girl at the airport and take her to Lee Vista Center."

"What happened?"

"She, well, she sort of disappeared."

"Did you check her room?"

"I kind of figured that out on my own."

"Good, good. We're on a roll. And when you did that, was her luggage still there?"

"Right where I left it."

"That would mean she's coming back, right?"

"I didn't think of that."

"I thought of that, too," Mike said.

"Why didn't you bring it up before, then?" I asked her.

"Because you just now told me about it, smartass," Neil said.

"Good point." I motioned for Mike to hush.

"Females, my friend. Everything she's got is in that suitcase. If she hasn't been kidnapped, she'll definitely come back."

"I was told she met a guy at the Vistana bar."

"There you have it, then. She's young, on her own, and met a guy. They could be in another room."

"His red Vette isn't in the parking lot."

"Maybe they went out for a bite."

"The Presidential has restaurants and a bar."

"Maybe it's too expensive there."

"We're talking *heiress*, my smart but sometimes slightly naïve buddy. She probably spends more on her nails than I spend on booze in a month."

"Maybe they wanted privacy."

"There's that, I guess."

"But you don't think so."

"It pisses me off that she disappeared. It makes me look bad."

"You mean, like a schmuck?"

"Exactly."

"And an idiot?"

"You really don't have to go into so much detail, Neil. . ."

"I can see how you're taking this the wrong way."

"I have to find out where she is."

"This guy that met her at the bar. Other than the Vette, what else have you got?"

"He's around thirty, six feet, medium build, and has blond hair His name might be Smith."

"Not much to go on."

"He's got a tatt on his neck that says 'Manta.'"

"Now *there's* something."

"I thought so, too."

Silence. "You still there?" I asked.

"Still here."

"I don't hear the wonderful clicking sound of your elegant fingers dancing on the keyboard."

"That's probably because I'm drinking coffee and scratching myself."

"Too much information. So why aren't you looking this up for me?"

"I'm waiting for the magic word."

"I have to *ask*?"

"We're busy here, Deacon. In case you haven't heard, this town is full of perverts, psychos, illegals."

"C'mon, Neil. I'm in hot water. My ass could be on the line."

"I hate when you whine. It's . . . unmanly." Neil grunted, as he usually did when he sat up. The clicking of his keyboard was music to my ears.

***

As Mike and I got back in the elevator and I thought more about the girl's suitcase, I felt a *little* better. Or at least not quite as bad.

Neil was right. Females protected their personal property as fiercely as a mother bear protects her cubs. They carried their makeup with them wherever they went. It was standard equipment. As important as an artist's satchel of paints and brushes.

The elevator door slid open. We stepped out. My cell buzzed. It was my mother.

Mom never failed to call at inappropriate times. Just a few weeks ago, she'd called when I was zip-tied to a chair and about to be tortured. She'd been cool about it, asking my torturer to let me talk to her, but it was still kind of embarrassing. Torture's no fun to begin with, but when your mother steps into the picture, the situation becomes even worse.

"Hi, Mom." Mike and I hurried down the hall. "I'm a little busy right now, but in case you're wondering, I'm doing fine."

"Ralphie, can't I *ever* call you when you're not busy?"

"Just pick a time when I'm not busy and sneak in a call. And don't call me Ralphie."

"Now you're being silly."

"Me? Silly?"

"Ralphie, why won't you come down here for a nice visit like you promised? It's been over a month now, and--"

"It's been *two weeks* since I promised, and don't call me Ralphie."

"Well, it seems longer. Your Uncle Nicky is waiting patiently for you to help him with his project. He can't do it himself, you know. He's over seventy now, and--"

"Why'd you call, Mom? I'm in the middle of something right now."

"Did you get the *biscotti* I sent you?"

"When'd you send them?"

"Three days ago. You should have them by now."

"I'll probably get them today or tomorrow."

63

"It's almost dinnertime. Didn't you pick up your mail yet?"

The only practical way of dealing with Mom was to make her believe everything was just fine, usually by lying. This was no big thing. I'd been lying to her since I was ten. "Now that you mention it, there was a package delivered this morning. I picked it up on my way out the door."

"Didn't you open it?"

"Didn't have time."

A maid wandered down the hall. I waved to get her attention.

"They won't keep very fresh in this heat," Mom said. "It's ninety-three here. I'll bet it's just as hot up there as well."

"Can you please open this door?" I asked the maid. "They gave me the wrong key at the desk and I'm having trouble finding someone down there to take me seriously."

She reached into her pocket.

"What's that, Ralphie? Something about a key?"

"Business, Mom. And don't call me Ralphie."

"I don't see why you hate your name so much. I've been calling you that since you were little."

"I know, and I really wish you'd stop doing it."

"I just don't see why a pet name should--"

"I'm almost *forty*, Mom."

"A mother never thinks of her son as--"

"The package is in an air-conditioned apartment. I'll open it when I get home."

"They're good, but nothing's like fresh."

"I'm sure they'll be fine."

64

The maid unlocked the door and hurried away.

"You can have the fresh stuff when you come for a visit," Mom said. "Plus lasagna, just the way you like them."

"Sounds good, Mom." I approached the door.

"It'll be a nice visit."

"I'll be down before you know it."

"I'm not getting any younger, you know."

"No one is, Mom. Not even those celebrities who keep getting facelifts and paying people to change their birth dates."

"Just promise me you'll come down the first chance--"

"I promise."

"And that you'll be careful playing those stupid cowboy and Indian games--"

"Cops and robbers."

"Whatever."

"I really have to go." I hung up and eased open the door.

Mike was already inside, standing in the middle of the empty foyer.

***

Neil called me back about twenty minutes later, as Mike and I were walking back to the TransAm.

"The suitcase is gone," I told him.

"You went back to the room?"

"The suitcase is gone."

"You said that. Did you check the rest of the suite?"

"Yeah. The damned suitcase is gone."

"You sound tense."

"It pisses me off that she slipped by me *again*."

"I hear you. But it does sound weird, her disappearing, then coming back while you're not there, snatching up the suitcase--"

"She didn't snatch up that damned suitcase."

"How do you know?"

"That damned thing weighs a ton."

"Females can surprise you. Besides, they're funny about their stuff."

"There's no way that girl picked up that damned suitcase and ran off with it."

"Deacon, females are a lot stronger than they--"

"We're talking *princess* here, Neil. Pampered. Spoiled. Plus, she doesn't go much more than a hundred pounds. That suitcase weighed nearly as much as she does."

"Don't you think you're exaggerating?"

"He thinks I'm exaggerating," I told Mike.

"Too bad you can't prove any of this," she said.

"Who're you talking to?" Neil asked.

"Listen. I was the one lugging it from the terminal all the way to the hotel. Damned thing popped a few of my favorite joints and half a dozen very sensitive vertebrae."

"Makes you wonder what she's carrying. And who were you talking to?"

"Myself. I had a peek earlier. Princess is a fitness nut. She's lugging around half a dozen pairs of glamour bells with her. About eighty pounds, total."

"And she let *you* carry the suitcase?"

"She *ordered* me to carry it. Said it was too heavy for her."

"And it was too heavy for *you* as well?"

Now I knew what my brain had been trying to tell me when I first started thinking about it. "You're absolutely right. If she's a fitness nut--"

"She'd be capable of lugging her weights around."

"Fitness nuts should be stronger than the rest of us mortals, shouldn't they?"

"This is beginning to smell."

"By the way, what did you find out about the tag on the Vette?"

"I looked up 'Manta' and came up with several variations on the word. Closest match was 'MNTA1.'"

"Belong to a red Vette?"

"You got it."

Chapter 6

Neil's information took me to downtown St. Cloud, to a plan of ranch houses off Thirteenth Street, two blocks south of 192.

I was alone. Mike had already disappeared by the time I reached the Osceola County line. No big thing, really, since she was dead and had to recharge her ectoplasm from time to time. I didn't panic or anything--although I'm usually a little miffed when she vanishes without a word. It's sort of like when you're talking to someone on the phone and they say, "Gotta go," then hang up without giving you the chance to ask what's going on. However, this case is slightly different, since the person you're talking to is dead, there's no phone involved, and she doesn't say anything before she vanishes. It used to bother me, but since she does it so often, I've gotten used to it.

192 takes you straight to the ocean in one direction and the theme parks in the other, making it even more hectic and tourist-crammed than Orlando. You can get behind more lost tourists in St. Cloud than you can ever find in Orlando. And with the number of eateries flanking this stretch, the traffic is just as congested as it is in the busiest areas of West Orlando.

The one-and-a-half-story yellow brick house was obviously well-maintained--the front yard mowed, the bushes trimmed neatly beneath the living room window. The red shutters looked fairly new. The red Spanish tile roof appeared to be in great condition. Two vehicles sat in the drive: a sparkling gray BMW and an older model tan Ford Ranger. But no red Corvette in sight.

I parked along the curb and stared at the place, considering my options. In my business, considering my options first always turned out to be a good move. Things went smoother and turned out much safer. You didn't end up dead or arrested, and you usually went home with all your body parts intact and still functioning.

Once I decided on my strategy, I walked right up to the front door and pressed the buzzer. Since it was the middle of the day, sneaking around and peeking in the windows would attract unwanted attention. Anyway, the vehicles in the drive told me someone was home, so the direct approach would probably be the most sensible.

My questions would have to be personal and direct. In other words, I'd have to be irritating. This in itself was nothing new. My profession dictated that I irritate people. I'm good at it. In fact, I enjoy it. I don't enjoy upsetting innocent people or infuriating the guilty so much that they try to kill me, but I do enjoy nudging rich, corrupt people off their pedestal. In this case, I had no idea who was doing what to whom. I also had no idea who was going to answer the front door. According to Neil, the tag MNTA1 corresponded to the brick house belonging to a Jason Alan Smith, age 56. Smith co-owned SmithCo & Associates, an industrial firm providing building materials for homes scheduled for distribution in hurricane-ravaged projects in the Central Florida area. SmithCo had started up their operation in late 2004, after several major storms had swept through Florida in one season.

Neil had learned that Smith had two sons and one daughter. The sons were thirty and twenty-eight, the daughter twenty-four. The daughter was married and living with her husband and two daughters in Tampa. The middle kid, George, was presently in the military, serving in the Middle East.

Alan, the oldest, listed his profession as Software Consultant. His tax return last year was based on a salary of $24,000. To me, this raised flags. If it was possible to own a sparkling new Corvette on such a meager salary, I'd have one sitting under a cover in the space beside my TransAm at the apartment complex.

Jason Alan Smith appeared to be legitimate. And since he had no criminal record and nothing on his sheet but three speeding tickets issued more than thirty years ago, I couldn't consider him directly involved in anything illegal. But I needed to know why his thirty-year-old was using his address. If the questioning went well, I also intended to find out how the boy could afford a Corvette. If he'd managed it legally, I was definitely interested. I'd still use the TransAm for business purposes. The Vette would be reserved for the weekends when I'd cruise the roads looking for babes. Babes loved making out in convertible Vettes.

The front door opened. The man filling the doorway was about six feet tall and portly, with a thick head of silver hair. His face was ruddy and full, his small, light-blue eyes veiny. He gripped a bottle of Heineken in his right hand. "Yes?" he asked in a soft, low-pitched voice.

"Mr. Smith?"

A nod.

"I'm sorry to bother you, but I'm Lester Mandrake, Attorney-At-Law." I'd learned long ago that when you tell people you're a detective, they tend to lie. To the average Joe, "detective" means "cop," and everyone lies to cops. Attorneys are different. People hate them but also fear them, and usually tell the truth to avoid trouble.

"Am I . . . in trouble?"

"No, sir." I produced one of my many cards. I flashed it quickly so he wouldn't have a chance to study it. It was probably the card Artie, the Roto-Rooter man, left the last time he unclogged my sink. I put it back in my wallet.

He stared past me. "You *sure* you're an attorney?"

I froze. It's unnerving when people can see through you. But it pays to keep your cool and stick with your story. I shrugged and patted my shirt. I'm sure he was referring to my casual dress. "Their dress code sometimes gets on my last nerve. Why do you ask?"

"That TransAm yours?"

"Sure is."

He shook his head. "Never met an attorney yet that doesn't drive a BMW. Or Caddie. Or Continental. Or Lexus."

"I've had that ride since I was a kid."

"How 'bout that?" He was still shaking his head. "An attorney with good taste. Never thought

71

I'd see it." This man had obviously known some attorneys in his day. "Why the visit?"

"I'm here to ask you one or two questions about a certain red Corvette that might have been in the vicinity of a traffic accident on 192 this morning. If so, the driver might be asked to act as a witness in the case."

He blinked. "A *red* Vette?"

"With the tag--" I reached into my pants pocket for my notepad.

"Manta One?" he asked, having a slug of Heineken.

I knew right then that this man didn't have anything to hide. "That sounds like it, yes."

Smith shrugged. "My son's car. Alan."

"I found my pen and started scribbling. "Your son . . . is he home right now?"

"I haven't seen him in three, maybe four weeks."

"He lives with you?"

"No, he . . . he lives on his own."

"Could you give me an address?"

"I would if he had one."

I gave him my furrowed brow look. It usually goes well with acting the part of an attorney. People expect attorneys to have furrowed brows.

"If you knew my son, you'd understand."

"Understand what?"

"Alan . . . he's sort of a free spirit. Even when he was a kid, he was always wandering off. I don't know how many times the wife and I had to go out at night and hunt him down so we could all have dinner together."

"Does that mean he doesn't have an address or phone?"

"He's got a cell phone--"

"Have the number?"

Smith shrugged. "That's another problem. He's either losing them or tossing them. He'll give me a number, but by the time I try using it, he's already got himself another phone."

"Convenient."

"How's that?"

"Just thinking out loud. Does he work?"

"Alan's a computer whiz. He's been in software since high school. Went to Rollins, majored in Computer Science--"

"Where's he work, Mr. Smith?"

"The Orlando Center Building. A&D Software Services, based out of Miami. He's been with them three years, now. One of their top men." He straightened and beamed a little.

"He must make quite a bit of money."

"Sure does. He's always buying news clothes, shoes--"

"Corvettes aren't cheap."

"Especially the one he's got."

"What's so special about it?"

"The color, for one thing. Dealer didn't have it in stock, so Alan slipped him some extra cash to speed up the process, to get a nice, blood-red one from another dealership."

"Money talks."

"Interior had to be light-blue, as well."

"Light-blue?"

73

"Alan hates black. Too hot. Can't blame him. Not in this heat."

Yeah, I had to find out how to get one of those babies. "How's he keep in touch?"

"How's that?"

"You know. Thanksgiving? Christmas? Birthdays? Doesn't he come home to see you and his mother?"

"His mom died, Mister--"

"Mandrake. Sorry to hear that."

He sighed and had a sip of beer. "Two years ago, now. Ovarian cancer."

"That's tough."

"Listen . . . I don't know how much I can help you--"

"That's all right. I'll look him up through his company."

"He's a good kid. Always wants to do the right thing."

"Like his daddy."

He grinned. And had another slug of beer.

***

I got back in the TransAm and called Neil.

"What'd you come up with?" he asked.

"The father's straight-arrow but I'm pretty sure his oldest son isn't."

"Go on. . ."

"He doesn't see his boy much. Apparently Junior likes being on his own, but he's a good boy, nonetheless. Dad's definitely proud of his son."

"That could mean several things. The father's not clean, for one thing."

"He seems legit to me."

74

"Then the father doesn't know what's going on."

"Junior doesn't live at home."

"If Daddy doesn't see his kid regularly, this keeps him out of whatever Junior's involved in."

"Junior also has no permanent address."

"So he registers his credit cards and car tag with his old man? That would be all right for an eighteen-year-old, but Junior's thirty. He work anywhere? All I could find was that tax return statement for last year."

"Kid works at A&D Software Services, based out of Miami."

Neil started clicking his keyboard. "A&D?"

"In the Orlando Center Building."

Neil stopped clicking. "Looks like a small outfit. A three-man operation."

"His dad said the kid's one of their top men."

"That's no stretch, with only two others in the company."

"What do they do?"

More clicks. "Contract work for several larger software companies in town. They handle overflow whenever the mother company's workload gets too much."

"Is that steady work?"

"It must be, if they're able to rent an office in one of the biggest skyscrapers in the downtown area. Know how much office space goes for nowadays?"

"How much?"

"A shitload. And they filed a tax return. Seems they generated over three million in revenues last year."

"From occasional sub work? That's a good gig."

"We're in the wrong business," Neil said.

"Something's not right. Junior's one of the three and he only grossed twenty-four grand. He should've grossed one-third of the three mill, less taxes and whatever else the company had to pay in."

"Either he does a ton of sack time or he's as stupid as a box of hair when collecting his paycheck."

"How many people do you know who are stupid about their paycheck? Even an idiot knows how much he's going to make. Besides, Daddy says he's a computer whiz."

"I know quite a few computer whizzes," Neil said. "Most are complete imbeciles about anything that doesn't involve a computer."

"Maybe. But something tells me Smith isn't an imbecile about anything."

"Call me silly, but I strongly suspect he made a little more than twenty-four grand last year."

"I intend to find out. And you *are* silly."

"That's rich, coming from you. So what about the girl?"

"Once I find Smith, I suspect I'll also find her."

***

Mike reappeared in the seat beside me as I drove west on 192. "Miss me?"

"Where were you? Recharging your batteries?"

"I was also talking to Flo."

"Flo?"

"A new friend."

"Dead or alive?"

"What do *you* think?"

"You have many of them?"

"Just a couple, so far. By the way, where are we going?"

"I have to find out more about Alan Smith."

"Did you find his father?"

"Nice guy."

"That's good, isn't it?"

"You don't want to meet nice people when you're digging up dirt. They get in the way, and when they do, they get hurt. In this case, I've got to look elsewhere. I've got an old contact who lives somewhere around here."

"Is he a cop?"

"Far from it. His name's Bud Hicks, but his first name's Herschel, although no one's called him that since grade school."

"What's wrong with Herschel?"

"You're not serious."

"What's wrong with it?"

"The same thing that's wrong with the name Rafaello."

"I like that name, too."

"You *are* serious, aren't you?"

She smiled impishly. "Always."

I met Bud by accident a few years back. He was picking pockets and his favorite haunt was the Kissimmee Arena. He made a good living working the tourists and locals until he screwed up and picked the pocket of a plainclothesman and spent two months in jail. The day he got out, he went back to the Arena and tried picking my pocket. I'd brought a prospective girlfriend on a casual date. When Bud targeted me, he didn't notice the uniform in the crowd just a few feet away until it was too late. He panicked, stumbling over his own two feet. And since his fingers were buried in my back pocket, I went down with him. I didn't bother telling the cop what happened. In my business, the more unsavory contacts you have, the better. Besides, Bud looked pitiful, sitting on the filthy floor near the cow pens, his clothes covered in straw and cow shit, his mouth bloody from where my elbow had connected. I didn't know whether to just leave him there or adopt him as a rescue. Since my date turned out to be a dud, I gave her money for a cab, drove Bud home, and cleaned him up.

Bud, of course, never forgot my kindness. Whenever my work took me to St. Cloud, I looked him up. Last I saw him, he was working in Walmart during the day and supplementing his income in bars and strip clubs on weekends. He assured me he no longer picks pockets, but I know better. It's in his blood, and he's good at it. His close call with me woke him up but didn't cure him. He's not really a bad guy. He takes only cash and always leaves the plastic.

Mike and I found Bud in Hardware helping a short, thickset woman about sixty-five find something among the shelves.

"He doesn't *look* like a crook," Mike said.

"That's how he gets away with doing what he does."

The lady waddled away, carrying a Stanley hammer and a small box of carpet nails. I snuck up to Bud and poked him between the shoulder blades. "All right, Louie, drop the gun," I whispered in my most sinister Humphrey Bogart voice.

He stiffened, then slowly turned around. It took him a second or two to recognize me, then another couple of seconds to catch his breath. It was probably because he'd expected Bogie to be standing there--although Bogie's been dead more than fifty years now. Even if he wasn't, he'd be wandering around in Hollywood--not St. Cloud. He'd also be extremely old, and wouldn't wander around without a walker or a couple of nurses carrying his oxygen tank.

Bud's color finally returned. He realized I wasn't Bogie and that I was just kidding. "Deacon?"

"No one else will admit to it."

"Shoulda known it was some funny guy."

"I guess you figured it out because Bogie's been dead all these years."

"Who?"

"Humphrey Bogart. The guy I just did."

"That was *Bogart*?"

"Incredible, huh? I need to forget detective work and do stand-up."

"Uh-huh."

"I guess I need to work on my Bogart."

"Why're you here, Deacon?" Bud was obviously less than dazzled and wanted to get down to business.

"You know anything about a guy named Alan P. Smith? He's thirty. About six feet tall. Light-brown hair."

A shrug.

"He drives a red convertible Corvette. He also has a tattoo on his neck that says Manta."

His small, veiny gray eyes narrowed. He hurried over to the counter, where a middle-aged woman studied the prices of paints on display. He tended to the female but kept sneaking a glance or two back at me.

"He knows Smith, doesn't he?" Mike asked.

"You know something? One day, you're gonna make a good detective."

"I'm dead."

"Hey, no one's perfect."

***

Five minutes later, Bud met me behind the tall stacks of a/c filters. Mike had wandered over to the Linen Department on the other side of the aisle. She was standing between a short, slender young woman and her cart, which was crammed with groceries, a box fan, a padded toilet seat, and a toddler. The kid sat in the cart, screaming and kicking the box with the fan. Mike was too preoccupied looking at a set of blue-gray bed linens to notice.

Bud kept glancing to his right, then his left, while groping for his cigarettes. As he fiddled with them, his ruddy color returned. Just thinking about his habit had apparently calmed him. I didn't know if it was Smith, the red Vette, or the Manta tatt that had spooked him.

"You're acting like someone slipped a live snake down your undershorts when you weren't looking," I said.

He just stuck a cigarette in his mouth and stuffed the crumpled pack back into his shirt pocket.

"You know you can't smoke in here, right?"

Groaning, he shoved the cigarette carefully through the hairy gray tuft above his left ear.

"Who's Smith? The local mob boss?"

He shook his head.

"The local hitter?"

No response.

"Work with me on this, okay? I'm lousy at charades and even worse at facial expressions. And I flunked Mind-Reading 101 the day I got married."

"This important?"

"It's a case I'm working on."

"Sure am glad I ain't you."

"You'd be surprised how many people have said that. I'm thinking of having a bumper sticker made."

"He's bad news. He works for a protection outfit in Kissimmee."

"In what capacity?"

"Howzat?"

"What exactly does he do?"

"Dunno, but he's bad news."

"You already said that."

"I've seen him around some strong-arm guys, work the door at the tittie bars."

"Does he carry?"

"You mean, like a gun?"

"That's pretty close to what I mean."

"I've seen him driving around some big dude. Hispanic. Word on the street says he's from Colombia. Name's Paseo. He takes money from the pawnshop owners, so they don't have to worry about being robbed."

"Let me guess. If they don't give him money, they're robbed?"

"Paseo's bad. And big."

"You mean he employs a lot of men? Or does he have trouble fitting into a thong bikini?"

Bud was not amused. When you're scared, you tend not to see the humor in things--not even if the quips are coming from a terrific stand-up guy like me. "A lotta guys," he said. "Some Hispanic, others locals."

"Know what Smith does, other than drive Paseo around?"

"Nope."

"Is Paseo the one who gave him the Vette?"

"Dunno."

"Have you heard about anything going down lately?"

He shrugged. I waited about ten seconds. Usually, when you wait ten seconds and no one says anything, it's because the meter has just run out. Bud was grateful to me for keeping him out of prison and never asked for money, but this business was obviously scaring him, so I slipped him twenty instead of my usual ten. He stared at it, so I gave him another twenty. "Ain't you scared, Deacon?"

"Don't I look scared?"

"Can't tell."

"It's my tough, devil-may-care good looks. But don't feel bad. My hard, unflinching exterior baffles even the best of crooks."

Bud frowned. "We're talking *bad guys* here. Hispanics. Kissimmee. Damn place is almost another Miami, for Chrissakes. You know. Chainsaws? Cuban neckties? Jumper cables? All sorts of scary stuff."

"The Cubans stole that necktie thing from the Italians. It used to be called the *Sicilian* necktie." It always bothered me that hoods were so stupid that they couldn't come up with their own ideas.

"They slit your throat--"

"I know the drill. From what I hear, it's not pleasant." I wasn't in the mood to worry about stuff like that.

He held up the bills. "You *sure* you wanna give me this?"

"I figure it might keep you away from the bars for a day or two. I don't want you picking pockets any more. You're too damned old for it."

Bud took one last glance up and down the aisle, then lowered his voice again. "Last I heard, Paseo's branching out."

"Into what?"

"Hookers."

"He's not already into that?"

"This is … high class stuff."

I hated when people didn't come to the point. "Speak plain, now. Make believe you're talking to an idiot."

He gave me a blank look.

"Not you--*me*. Just tell me what Paseo is branching into. I'll try and figure out the rest on my own."

"Word is, Paseo's running escorts."

Chapter 7

Mike joined me as soon as I went back outside. "You didn't buy anything?" I almost expected to see her carrying a white bag.

"Very funny."

"Why were you looking at bed linens?"

"Flo asked me to check out their latest supply next time I went to Walmart."

"Flo's dead, right?"

"So?"

"Why would anyone who's dead care about bed linens?"

Mike shrugged. "It's something to talk about when we get together. Besides, she's got relatives who are still alive. They like to keep up on the latest bargains."

"I guess I should've thought of that." My cell buzzed. It was Phil again. I'd hoped she wouldn't call this soon. I'd just found out some pretty frightening stuff. The way it looked, the girl had gone to the Vistana for a drink. Smith, working for Paseo, was probably on the lookout for fresh meat for their new escort service. Paseo would want young, good-looking, independent girls. Jackie Frazier would be the perfect choice. But I was just guessing and had to keep this to myself.

"What's happening?" I asked in my usual cheerful manner.

"You found out something, didn't you? It's bad, isn't it?"

"What makes you say that?"

"It's how you just answered the phone."

"I was being cheerful."

"You're being evasive."

"How'd you come up with *that*?"

"That's your evasive tone. You've found out something awful and you're trying to cover it up by being cheerful and funny."

"Me? Cheerful? Funny?"

"Ralph. . ."

"I didn't find out much. Not enough to come up with a decent conclusion. And certainly not enough to find the girl."

"Where are you?"

"Right now?"

"Yes, Ralph. As opposed to where you were ten minutes ago, and where you'll be ten minutes from now."

"Why the attitude? I'm answering your questions."

"This is very upsetting for me."

"I understand."

"So . . . where are you?"

"St. Cloud."

"What are you doing *there*?"

"Doing detective stuff. I thought you knew that."

A sigh. "What I mean is, why St. Cloud?"

"The guy who picked her up has a St. Cloud address."

"And you think Jackie might have gone there with him?"

"It's a possibility." We reached the TransAm and got in. Thank God, it wasn't as hot as before. Possibly because it was cloudy at the moment.

"Do you think you'll be able to find her fairly quickly?"

"I'm doing the best I can."

My passenger door opened. I was about to ask Mike how she could do that when a dark-haired guy around twenty-five slid right in and slammed the door. He appeared to be Latino, but with much darker coloring. He was dressed in jeans, a blue tee shirt, and black athletic shoes. He was fairly good-looking in a "bad boy" sort of way, with angry dark eyes and a couple of short parallel white scars marking his left cheek.

"I think we just picked up a hitchhiker," Mike said from the back seat.

"Looks like it."

The black butt of a small automatic protruding from his waistband instantly grabbed my attention. He didn't bother with it at the moment--which was a good thing. He just sat there, watching me. He wasn't grinning. He wasn't doing anything. An armed man getting into your car uninvited would freak out most folks. When you snoop around for a living, you tend to upset people. The more questions you ask, the more people you piss off. Sending an armed kid after you comes with the territory.

"Ralph? Still there?"

"I gotta go."

"Following a lead?"

"Actually, a lead followed me."

My passenger pointed to the cell phone. Using his index finger, he traced an imaginary line across his throat. Even a straight-laced, upstanding guy like me knows what that gesture means.

"I think you'd better do as he says," Mike said. "I can probably tickle his ear or something, but I'll be useless if he just up and shoots you."

"Something come up?" Phil asked.

"In a manner of speaking."

"What's going on?"

"I seem to have a guest at the moment."

"Ralph, what are you talking--"

"Like I said, I gotta go." I nodded to my new passenger. "Right?"

He also nodded but said nothing. He obviously didn't want Phil to hear his voice.

"I'll call you back." I pocketed the cell. My Beretta .380 sat comfortably in its black Uncle Mike's holster in the console between us. I didn't want to take it into the store for obvious reasons. I wondered, briefly, if I was fast enough to open the console, reach inside, grab the gun, yank the Velcro flap to remove it from its holster, flick off the safety, and point it at my passenger before he could pull his out of his waistband.

"Please don't," Mike said uneasily.

I glanced at her. Sometimes she was scary, reading me like that.

"I can tell by your eyes what you're thinking. Hold on. I might be able to distract him later."

"What's next?" I asked.

He pointed to the wheel.

"Want me to drive?"

He nodded. I wanted to ask him if he really could talk. Maybe he didn't speak English. Hispanics don't normally bother learning our language. They didn't think they need to. "Where to?"

"Letcha know," he said in a soft, bored voice.

His English was good--what there was of it.

"And if I say I've got other things to do?"

He pointed to his gun.

"Are you pointing to your gun? You're not funny or anything? That *is* a *gun*, right? Or are you just happy to--"

In a twinkling, he'd uncrossed his arms and snapped his right wrist. The gun was out, cocked, held dead-steady, and pointing directly at my right eye. Just like that. This kid was lightning-fast. I'd been watching him closely and hadn't even seen the gun leave his waistband. Good thing I hadn't tried going for the Beretta.

"Yep. It's a gun, all right."

He gestured with it and didn't tuck it away until I'd flicked on the ignition.

"I think you'd better do as he says," Mike said.

"Well, since I've got nothing else to do right now, I think I can manage that."

***

As instructed, I drove west on 192.

My passenger stared straight ahead, his hands resting on his thighs. I knew better than waste my time thinking about my Beretta. Even if the boy nodded off, I still probably couldn't get to it fast enough. And if I did, the end result would be disastrous. Especially since I was driving. But even if I could get to my gun, I wouldn't be able to shoot him. He was a *kid*, for God's sake. He probably still lived with his mom. I could even see acne scars on his neck, just beneath his jaw.

He wore a gun, knew how to take it out quickly, and obviously worked for a bad guy. But he was still a kid. And I was no killer. I couldn't put this boy's lights out. But despite the circumstances, I didn't think I was in much danger of being killed. Junior didn't appear crazy enough to kill me while I drove. If he'd wanted me dead, he would've already done the deed.

Someone obviously wanted to talk to me. If this someone wanted me dead, escorting me quietly out of town was not the best way to do it. And they would never have let me drive. A troublesome victim is usually knocked out, taken somewhere remote, and shot.

I had to do what he said and hoped my instincts were right. It bothered me that I'd been spotted so quickly. If Alan Smith worked for Paseo, and Paseo was as paranoid as most other key crime figures I knew of, the Smith home was probably under daily surveillance. And if Paseo's organization was large enough, if wouldn't be difficult to send someone after me.

But even if the Smith home was being staked out, how would Paseo know about me? Alan Smith never saw me before, so why would he or anyone else consider me a threat?

That might be what this was all about. Paseo didn't know about me, so this might be his way of finding out who I was. His calling card. This didn't make sense. If Bud was right about Paseo taking over just recently, my being spotted and picked up so quickly meant high-caliber power. And connections.

"You really get in trouble a lot," Mike said from the back seat.

"I know."

My passenger glanced at me.

"Want me to try talking to him?" Mike asked.

"What would you say?"

The boy frowned.

"I'd tell him not to shoot you, but it would probably scare him. People can do stupid things when they're scared."

"Like shoot me?"

"It's a possibility."

We reached the major intersection at 192 and South Orange Blossom. As usual, traffic was murder. The dinner hour always plays havoc with Florida's roads. Today proved no exception. Lanes of out-of-state cars, trucks, RVs, and motor homes clogged each artery of the intersection. I stopped at the light. My passenger still stared straight ahead, but I could tell he kept me locked in his peripheral vision.

"Try talking to him," Mike said.

I shrugged.

"It might break the ice."

"You think so?"

"He might even appreciate your wonderful personality."

She could be right. A little pleasant conversation could go a long way. Besides, camaraderie never hurt. "Live around here?" I asked.

No response.

"Work in Kissimmee?"

Nothing.

"In case you were wondering, I went to UCF, where I got my BA. Took me five years, but I was really in no hurry. I met some hot chicks there, too. That was a while ago. You were probably still crawling around then, drooling and soaking your diapers. How old are you, by the way? Twenty-one? Sorry if that's way off, but I'm really lousy at guessing ages."

Silence. So much for camaraderie, and my wonderful personality. The light changed. He pointed straight ahead.

"Maybe he's self-conscious about his English," Mike said.

"You honestly think that's an issue?" I said as I eased forward with the flow.

Junior turned to gawk at me. He was probably wondering why I was smiling. *Loco*, he no doubt thought. *Just another crazy Anglo.*

I knew I'd better explain this. Otherwise, Junior might shoot me and tell his boss he did it because I was a dangerous nutcase. "Just thinking out loud," I said, shrugging.

He went back to watching the road ahead.

"You know where we're going?" Mike asked.

"Let me find out. Where are we going?" I asked Junior.

He pointed straight ahead.

"I guess that means Kissimmee," I said.

He nodded.

"He probably works for that man Paseo," Mike said. "The one your friend warned you about."

"Possibly."

Junior kept glaring.

"Just making an observation."

Junior continued to glare.

"I need something to pass the time," I said. It's best to act stupid in such circumstances. As anyone who knows me will tell you, I'm an expert at acting stupid. My tactic worked. He scratched the back of his neck, then shrugged and sat back in his seat.

"You're probably going to meet him," Mike said.

"I've already guessed we're not headed for Space Mountain."

Junior shook his head.

"Or *are* we?"

"Quiet."

"You don't like my thinking out loud?"

"Quiet."

"I get nervous when I'm with someone who won't talk to me."

No reply.

"You have a gun, too. That makes me even *more* nervous."

"You really know how to talk your way out of trouble," Mike said.

"And into it," I said.

Junior glanced in Mike's direction as if he suspected someone was really sitting there.

"I have a guardian angel," I told him. Sometimes it pays to be honest.

93

He blinked.

"That's who I've been talking to."

He snuck another glance toward the back.

"She's sitting right behind me."

Junior watched me. He seemed to be trying to determine if I was feeding him a crock, or just planning something. People get all nervous and bent out of shape when they have no idea what you're up to.

"She's really a knockout," I said. "I mean *smoking*."

"Oh, stop." Mike lowered her head. I could tell she was getting embarrassed.

"She's a brunette," I told Junior. "With a body a guy dreams about."

"You dream about my body?" she asked.

"You really need to ask?"

"Quiet," Junior said.

"You need to start taking this seriously," Mike said. "This could turn ugly."

I nodded. "Okay."

Mike moved closer. She rested her non-existent forearms on the back of the seat so her bracelets showed clearly on her smooth, tanned non-existent flesh. "You're probably being taken somewhere private," she said. "Paseo probably wants to know why you were questioning Alan Smith's father."

"Possibly."

"I suggest you cooperate. If Paseo believes you're not a threat, he might leave you alone."

"That would be nice, but so far, he's doing a lousy job."

Junior squinted.

94

"I'm nervous, dammit," I told him.

Junior scowled at the back seat again.

"Some people pray," I told him. "I talk to my angel. It helps when I'm scared. Ever been scared?"

His blank look didn't reassure me.

***

Two blocks later, Junior pointed to the left lane.

I flicked on my blinkers and waited for my chance. As soon as the gap presented itself, I pulled into the next lane, and he pointed to the turnoff lane. "Let me take a wild stab at this. You want me to turn off." He continued pointing. "Life's *so* much more pleasant when you understand your fellow man." Then I did as ordered.

Half a block later, he pointed toward my left. I made a left at the corner, where a half-filled 7-Eleven, a crowded Wendy's, and a busy tune-up shop anchored the block.

"Want to stop at Wendy's for a double cheese and fries?" I asked. "I haven't eaten since breakfast."

Junior said nothing.

We passed several old-fashioned one-story houses that had been converted into barbershops, flower shops, insurance agencies, and antique stores. As we went farther south, young Hispanics appeared along the curb and at street corners, staring as we passed. Three blocks later, a residential neighborhood extended for several blocks. Skinny dark-haired boys played tag with one another. Others wrestled on the grass in someone's front yard. Young girls played hopscotch on the cracked walk. Teens shuffled along in pairs

95

and threesomes, sharing cigarettes, joints, and lines of coke.

"Is this your neighborhood?" I figured I'd give camaraderie one last stab. "If you're taking me to your home for supper, we should've stopped somewhere. I could've bought a nice bottle of table wine."

Junior said nothing.

"You drink wine, don't you?"

Silence.

"I'd feel guilty, showing up at your house without--"

"Shuddup."

A block beyond the subdivision, several large aluminum storage buildings and warehouses came into view. Junk cars, RVs, and motor homes faced the street, nearly obscuring the weathered buildings behind them.

"Pull over," Junior said.

Weeds and tall grass took over just a few feet from the edge of the narrow two-lane road. Beyond that, a wide ditch at least three feet deep looked like it was just waiting to devour a good-sized TransAm for supper. "There isn't any room for me to--"

"Pull over." His hand moved toward his gun.

I pulled off the road and coasted carefully into the weeds, stopping about a foot short of the ditch. There was no traffic, which made me feel more vulnerable. Junior pushed open the door, slammed it shut, and crossed in front of the TransAm. He opened my door. "Move over."

I slid over to the passenger side. Junior got behind the wheel. He reached into his back pocket, pulled out a scrap of thin black material, and tossed it in my lap. I picked it up. It was a hood, of course. Standard headgear for an abduction, or a trip into enemy territory. "What's this?" I knew what it was but decided to act stupid again.

"Put it on."

"It's a *hood*." I know that statement made me sound like a moron, but I couldn't help it. I hated hoods. They were dark and confining. Some even smelled funny or had lint that got in your nose and mouth. This one had just come out of a psycho kid's back pocket--who knew what he'd been sitting on before he jumped into my car?

"I can't do this," I said.

He continued to stare.

"I *hate* hoods."

His hand moved toward his gun.

"It'll mess up my *hair*. . ."

The gun was suddenly out, cocked, and pointed at my right eye. What was it about my right eye that fascinated this asshole?

"I think you'd better put it on," Mike said.

"I don't think I have a choice."

"Don't worry. I'll pay attention."

"Just don't go off looking for bargains with Flo again." I pulled the hood open, closed my eyes to make the process less traumatic, then held my breath while fitting it gently over my head. Once it was on, I opened my eyes, shivering at the blackness. I closed my eyes again.

The TransAm eased back onto the road.

Chapter 8

Junior drove straight, then made a left.

"One block," Mike said, close to the hood covering my head.

We went straight for about a minute, made a right, then drove straight.

"Two blocks, and it looks like he'll be going straight a ways."

I tried determining where we'd gone, but even with Mike's directions, it's kind of difficult when you're wearing a hood. The total darkness not only engulfs you, it interferes with your equilibrium. Besides, I wasn't familiar with this area. For a while I tried picking up scents, but all I could distinguish was a trace of honeysuckle--which told me I was in Florida. I already knew that.

After one last left turn, Junior pulled off the road, eased up a slight incline, went a few yards, then brought the TransAm to a sudden stop. He switched off the engine, put the brake on, then got out and slammed the door.

"It's some sort of auto body shop," Mike said. "There's a grove of trees behind the building. I don't see a sign, but there are all sorts of cars, low-riders, and engine blocks toward the back."

My door squealed open. A hand roughly grabbed my upper arm and pulled. I got out and my door slammed shut beside me. The hand continued gripping my arm, coaxing me forward. I proceeded cautiously, hoping Junior wouldn't be a butthole and trip me or force me into a wall. I could rely on

Mike up to a point, but I had no choice but let myself be led.

The trip, thankfully, was short. We walked five paces and stopped. A blast of air-conditioning brushed my arms. I stepped through a threshold and into more air-conditioning. The floor felt solid, like concrete--which told me Mike was right about it being an auto body shop. It had the feel and smell of a warehouse.

It's frightening when you're being led around blind. You have the strange feeling you and the other person are the only beings in the universe. It could be a pleasant, bonding type of experience if the other person is someone you like and respect. But if the person is someone you don't know, doesn't speak much, and has already threatened you with his gun, the experience is far from pleasant. I didn't hear any other footsteps or voices--just the constant hum of the air-conditioning. I counted another fifteen steps. We rounded a corner, went three more steps, and stopped. A door opened. We went through.

"Offices," Mike whispered.

The hand gripping my arm vanished. Something cold and hard--a gun barrel? --prodded me firmly in the small of my back. Not knowing what else to do, I moved forward. The gun prodded me again. I took five steps. A door closed behind me.

"Turn right," a soft, low-pitched voice said. The pressure on my spine disappeared. I turned. A hand pressed against my chest, shoving me backward, into something soft and comfortable. A chair. So far, so good. If they had plans to kill me, they wouldn't let me sit in a chair, they'd shoot me and dump my body. And they certainly wouldn't have bothered with the hood.

Due to my temporary blindness, I had no idea if Junior was still in the room, or if there were others. If they had guns. Or knives. Or carried chainsaws. Seeing *Scarface* many years ago didn't help my anxiety very much. But I did suspect someone was standing behind me. I wanted to pull off the hood, but knew that wouldn't score points here. When someone goes to such lengths to make sure you can't see him, he's not going to let you change the program.

A low-pitched, heavily accented voice directly in front of me said, "What's your name?"

"Deacon."

"Deacon what?"

"Ralph's my first name."

"Whaddya do, Deacon?"

"You mean for a living?"

"That's what I mean."

One thing was in my favor. I was doing this as a personal favor for Phil--which meant she really wasn't my client. In other words, I wasn't obliged to stay ethical and keep quiet. I was a professional, but I wouldn't risk my life protecting a foul-mouthed, spoiled bitch who called my classic ride a piece of junk. But I couldn't help thinking that telling them the truth could be a huge mistake. Crooks lead a life based on lies. Truth scares them. Crime bosses believe only in what works for them. *Their* truth is what they live by.

"I'm a private detective," I said.

A heavy sigh. A finger of ice poked me between the shoulder blades. That sigh scared me. It told me this man didn't like detectives. Hoods usually didn't, but you couldn't blame them. No one likes some stranger poking around, looking for trouble.

"What were you doing at the Smith residence?"

"Asking questions about his son."

"Why?"

"I'm trying to find a girl."

"What girl?"

"A girl I picked up at the airport."

"Who is she?"

"Her name is Jackie Frazier. I was supposed to take her to the hotel."

"Why?"

"As a favor to my ex-wife."

"Favor?"

"A client of hers is having a birthday party tomorrow. His wife wanted their daughter to be their surprise guest."

"Which hotel did you take her to?"

"The Presidential, at Lee Vista Center."

"Did you?"

"Did I what?"

"Take her."

I nodded.

"It is dark in this room," he said. "I cannot hear if you nod or shake your head."

I wanted to tell him to put on this damned hood if he really wanted to see dark. But I knew better. "I nodded."

101

"If you took her, why the questions?"

"She disappeared."

"You just said you took her."

"I did."

"Then why you looking for her?"

"I promised my ex-wife I'd drop off the girl at the hotel, but when I took her suitcase up to her room, she'd already disappeared."

Silence.

"He's thinking it over," Mike said. She'd appeared slightly to my right. I could tell she was close.

"You told your ex-wife this girl disappeared," the voice said.

"Yeah."

"Stupid."

"I know."

"What're you doing with your ex-wife?"

I shrugged. "We're friends."

A long pause. Then: "You're *friends* with your ex-wife?"

That always fascinated people. Everyone expects you to remain mortal enemies after the divorce. "I know it sounds weird--"

"You're *friends* with a woman you used to fuck?"

"We were also friends when we were . . . when we were married."

"You were *friends* with your *wife*?"

"It's complicated."

I heard the click of a lighter. The room quickly grew pungent with cigar smoke. The suffocating hood grew even worse when the smoke leaked inside. I stifled a cough.

"Deacon, get out of town and stop asking questions."

"What should I do first?"

Another sigh. Movement behind me. Something hard swatted me on the back of the head. I slumped forward and massaged my stinging skull. The weapon felt familiar. Probably because I'd been hit with one before. It was probably a rolled-up magazine.

"Don't be a smartass, Deacon. I don't like smartass."

"I'll try."

"You work with the cops?"

"Only when I have to."

"Why?"

"Why what?"

"Why only when you have to?"

"I'm not too wild about cops." Neil was my friend, and cops were good to have on your side from time to time, but I really didn't get along with them very much.

"Why not?"

"They're assholes."

I thought I heard a soft snicker.

"And they have attitudes. And too many rules. They're always getting in the way."

"You're a cop."

"I'm a detective."

"What's the difference? You both get in the way."

"I only get in the way when someone's paying me. Or when someone's in trouble and needs a favor."

"Where's your office?"

"Orlando."

"Go back to your office. And stop asking questions."

"Then you don't know about this girl?"

"I *said*, stop asking questions."

This time, the magazine caught me at the base of the neck. This blow was much more painful and twice as effective. An army of warm tingling fluttered across my shoulders and down my arms. I massaged my neck and waited for the tingling to go away. I sure was glad I was being questioned on an empty stomach. Throwing up inside a hood would be a huge bummer. I'd have to take the hood off so I wouldn't choke to death, then use it to wipe my face. They'd probably shoot me while I was cleaning up, and I'd be found with throw-up all over me. Phil would be upset. So would I.

"Understand this time?"

"Sure, but I've still got to find that girl--"

"You don't listen too well, do you?"

"It's never been one of my better qualities."

"Asking questions will get you killed."

"I know."

"But you still do it."

"Asking questions is part of my job."

"Take my advice and don't ask so many. You'll live longer."

"I can go, then?"

Silence. "He's thinking," Mike said. "But I'd keep from saying much more if I were you."

"Lemme ask *you* a question," the figure said.

"Go right ahead."

"You the same Deacon, Old Man Raguzzo put the word out about?"

"I'm the only Deacon I know of. What word is that?"

"Hands off."

"Really? He said that?"

"He said it, but I don't like it. Not one fucking bit."

"He told me he was going to. I didn't think he'd do it, though."

"Why not?"

"He's a bad guy."

"Raguzzo's a man of his word."

"You and he friends?"

"Never met the man. We're competitors, but he keeps his word. I respect men who keep their word."

"Why don't you like the hands off? All I'm doing is trying to find--"

"You're asking questions. I don't like questions. You ask questions, people pay attention. I don't want people paying attention. I like people much better when they're acting stupid and not getting in my way. I don't like cops, neither. If it wasn't for Raguzzo, you'd be filling up a sinkhole. Got it?"

"I think so."

"Just remember one thing. Hands-off only works as long as I decide to honor it. Right now, you're a small pain in the ass. A zit. You know what happens to zits?"

I tried a wild guess. "They get popped?"

"*Bueno*. You ain't so *stupido*. I like that. You're okay for a zit. You become a carbuncle? That's when I've got to have you lanced. I've got *lots* of lancers. Three of them are in this room. And they're bored." Another slim plume of smoke drifted in my direction. I didn't want to piss him off again, so I held in the next cough. Then I felt movement in front of me. Something pressed firmly against my face. I tried pulling back, but another hand grabbed the back of my head and kept me from moving. I caught a whiff of something sweet and minty just before I realized I was being chloroformed. I made a brief attempt to struggle, but someone grabbed my right hand as well as my left. Everything turned black quickly.

Chapter 9

I woke up and found myself enveloped in darkness.

Traffic sounds drifted into my ears. I was lying on a narrow seat. It was firm but didn't feel like a couch. I experimented with my left palm. Upholstery. Smooth. Cracked and taped in a couple of places. Vinyl? Leather? My TransAm? Everything was so *dark*. I couldn't see a damned thing.

I pushed myself up. My right side buzzed with painful numbness. I'd obviously been in the same position for quite a while. I lay back. The numbness grew--an army of hot pinpricks jabbing my flesh from my shoulder down to my thigh. When the sharp pain ebbed into a heavy swell of throbbing warmth, I moved my shoulders and arms to get the blood moving again. But I still saw nothing. Panic sliced through me. "Those assholes blinded me." My voice sounded muffled.

"Take off the hood, silly," Mike said.

I reached up to touch my face. She was right. That damned hood. Feeling genuinely stupid, I yanked it off, pulling a clump of hair along with it. I cringed at the unexpected twinge of pain. But at least I could see. And the familiarity of the interior of the TransAm caused a billow of warmth to envelop me. Mike sat in front, grinning over the seat at me. I should've been pissed, but since everything had turned out okay, I sighed in relief.

Nausea quickly took over. A rumbling in my stomach made me gag. I wanted to throw up. I pushed open the door, stuck my head out, and coughed weakly.

"Are you okay?" she asked.

"Do I look okay?"

"That *was* silly of me, wasn't it?"

That minor effort exhausted me. I wiped my mouth with my forearm, then lay face-down, staring at the squashed cigarette butts and the smashed gum wrappers littering the filthy pavement less than two feet below my face. I tried remembering what happened. It came back slowly--lazy images mixed in with the heavy fog. The hood. The soft, heavily accented voice. I'd been talking to Paseo. And when he'd finished with me, someone shoved something minty and mediciny into my face. Everything went dark.

"Where are we?"

"Walmart."

"Which one? There are only a zillion of them."

"St. Cloud. That Smith guy came into the room right after they'd knocked you out. Paseo asked him a few questions--mostly the same stuff he asked you."

"Smith say anything?"

"Hardly anything, actually. He didn't recognize you when they took off your hood."

"I don't believe he's ever seen me."

"That's probably what saved you. It convinced Paseo you were telling the truth. He told the kid who brought you to take you back to your car, drive back to St. Cloud, and leave you there."

108

"I'm surprised Smith didn't lie."

"He's afraid of Paseo. Everyone in the room seemed to be Paseo's the type who can tell if you're lying. He's very intimidating."

Footsteps. A young voice a few feet to my right said, "Shitfaced, man?"

Two people had stopped about five feet away. A guy and a chick. Both were skinny and around eighteen, with a glazed look in their eyes. A heavy whiff of weed wafted over. My eyes watered. They stood side by side, the girl playing with her long, dirty-blond hair. The guy wore a baggy red sweatshirt, loose pants, and scuffed athletic shoes. The girl wore a short crop-top that showed off her silver navel ring. She also wore shorts and flip-flips. Her skinny arms and legs were covered with tatts.

"What was your first clue?" I tried pushing myself up.

"Better cool it, man," he said. "Cops come here all the time. They'll haul your ass in, you upchucking like that."

"Thanks. I'll remember that the next time I decide to upchuck."

"Nice ride. man."

I always thought it refreshing when the younger generation showed evidence of good taste. "Thanks."

"What is it? A hundred years old?"

I always thought it disgusting when the younger generation showed you how stupid they actually were. "You're a moron."

"You don't have to be nasty, man."

"Yeah, I do. I really do."

"Got money?" He held out a palm.

I reached into my pocket. My slim wad remained in there. I was surprised Junior hadn't rolled me. Wonders never cease. I pulled my hand out empty. "Yeah, I do."

"You're *really* nasty, man."

"Uh-huh," the girl said, still twirling her hair.

"You are, you know," Mike said.

"Don't encourage them," I said.

"Who you talking to, man?"

"The tooth fairy. Now go home and remind your mothers how silly they were to want children."

They shuffled away, mumbling.

"The tooth fairy?" Mike asked.

"Give me some slack. I've had a rough day." With a grunt, I let my legs fall to the floor and heaved myself into a sitting position. The nausea returned. Gripping the open door, I pulled myself into a standing position. The parking lot shifted, swayed, then rocked. I closed my eyes and waited for the world to settle down. I managed to close the door, heaved open the front door and collapsed onto the front seat. I lay there, my head on the console, willing myself to recover. Vaguely I wondered where Mike was. "Am I lying on top of you?"

"You can't do that to a spirit."

"Where are you, then?"

"Floating right above your face."

The image cleared some of the fog in my head. "Boy, am I glad you're dead."

"Why?"

"Use your imagination."

"You're half-dead and still thinking of sex?"

"What can I say? I'm funny that way." As the nausea subsided, I opened my eyes. Keys dangled from the ignition. "They didn't touch anything?"

"They just put you in back and brought you here. Then they got out and left you."

I pushed myself up and opened the console. The Beretta lay inside. Since Mike said they didn't mess with it, I didn't bother checking it. I pulled the door shut. Then, mindful of the console, I slid across the seat and situated myself behind the wheel. Mike had already drifted through me and over to the passenger's side. My nausea returned, bringing with it a heavy thumping between my temples. I rode it out.

"Feeling better?"

"Do I look like I do?"

"Actually, you look pretty bad."

"Hey, thanks."

"You're welcome. So what are you going to do now?"

"Sit here for a little while and try to figure out what I've learned over the last few hours."

"Sounds impressive. Professional."

"Actually, I need the time to recuperate from that shit they shoved in my face."

"That'll work, too. What have you figured out so far?"

"I strongly suspect Paseo has never heard of Jackie Frazier."

"I got that when he was talking to Alan Smith. Smith didn't say too much or volunteer any information. Anyone could tell he was nervous. He was obviously hiding something."

111

"I don't think Paseo's interested in kidnappings. Since he hasn't been in this country long, he wouldn't have had the time to engineer anything while organizing an escort operation. Crime figures generally target corporate leaders, drug kingpins--high-profilers with clout and limitless resources. John Frazier's rich, but probably not important enough to warrant kidnapping his daughter."

"Do you know this for a fact?"

"If Frazier does business with Phil, you can bet he's legit. Phil's much too uptight and law-abiding to deal with anyone even remotely suspicious."

"That makes sense."

"Paseo wouldn't bring great risk upon himself or his organization with something that would not only bring in the cops, but also the Feds. Escorting is a glamorized version of prostitution. It's accepted more than regular prostitution because it caters to high profilers. And as long as everyone stays fat and happy, nothing usually goes wrong."

"Still, you'd think Paseo would know everything Smith's involved in."

"Smith works for Paseo. He isn't married to him. Smith has no special allegiance to anyone but himself. And as I'd learned over the years, there really is no honor among thieves. But if Smith is kidnapping women for white slavery trafficking or to provide escorts for Paseo's service, he's facing federal prosecution. I have to find Smith, but without getting too close to Paseo."

"That'll be tough."

"That's where you come in." My cell buzzed. It was Phil. "What's happening," I said.

"Where have you been? I've been trying to call you for *two hours*."

"Two hours?"

"I must've tried your line ten times, Ralph. Where were you? Trying to avoid me again?"

"Now why would I do that?"

"You found out something bad. Why else wouldn't you answer your phone?"

"That's not exactly what happened. . ."

"What *did* happen?"

"I've been here."

"Where is here?"

"Where I am."

"Ralph, I'm not in the mood for your jokes. It's been a long, exhausting day. I'm tired and upset. I haven't heard from you and was worried. You did say you had company when we last talked. That was three hours ago. Ordinarily, something like that wouldn't worry me, but in your case, with those horrible people you're always dealing with--"

"Actually, I just woke up."

I heard her gasp. "You've been *sleeping*?"

"In a matter of speaking."

A pause. "You're telling me you've been *sleeping* while I've been worried half to death about--"

"The nap wasn't my idea. I've been . . . sort of unconscious."

Silence. I knew that would get her. Whenever you're being badgered by an angry woman, just tell her you've been unconscious. Or that you were

113

beaten up. It's the best get-out-of-trouble card I can think of.

"Ralph, you're either unconscious or you're not. That's like saying you're sort of pregnant."

"I'm not pregnant. But I *was* unconscious."

"Are you all right? What happened? Should I call someone?"

"Phil, calm down."

"I've been half-sick with worry all day, wondering why you haven't been answering your phone, if you're even *alive*--"

"I'm alive."

"But you were unconscious. . ."

"You're still worried about me. That's refreshing."

"This is nothing to joke about. Tell me what happened. You were really . . . *unconscious*?"

"That's what they tell me."

I heard the flick of a cigarette. She'd probably gone through a full pack in the last two hours. I could imagine her pushing her long black hair away from her face as she paced the living room. I wondered what she was wearing. Probably her bathrobe, with just her bra and panties on underneath. When something troubled her, she never bothered keeping the bathrobe tied. She just marched around the apartment with it flapping open. Phil was quite fetching when annoyed. But this wasn't the right time to ask what she was wearing.

"Tell me what happened. Please?"

"Where should I start?"

"At the beginning."

114

"Okay, it's like this. My ex-wife called this morning to--"

"Stop being cute and tell me what happened."

"This kid--he's around twenty or so--got in my car when I was talking to you and told me exactly where to go."

"He just happened to know what you were doing?"

"Obviously."

"And he knew where to *find* you?"

"I know this might sound a little confusing--"

"*Confusing* isn't the word I'd use, Ralph. You're saying this kid just got in your car, gave you directions . . . and you automatically did as he said?"

"His gun convinced me to do as he said."

"He . . . had a *gun*?"

"Looked like a Sig Sauer. Or maybe a Makarov. It was probably a three-eighty. They're compact, easy to handle--"

"He pointed a *gun* at you?"

"I wouldn't have gone anywhere with him if he hadn't. What kind of jerk do you think I am?"

"Ralph, he *kidnapped* you."

"Really? I thought he was just a tad obsessive about being alone with me."

"Ralph. . ."

"I know. Can the smartass."

"Please."

"The other guy didn't like it, either."

"*What* other guy?"

"The crime boss I talked to."

"You were talking to a *crime* boss?"

115

I didn't want to tell Phil about Alan Smith. The less she knew, the better. I shouldn't have told her about Paseo, but she'd given me no choice. "I figured he'd probably want to know what was happening on his turf."

"But . . . wasn't that kind of risky?"

"Me? Take risks?"

"Ralph, *please* stop. . ."

"I have to do a *lot* of risky things in this business, Phil."

"I know. It's why we're divorced, isn't it?"

"One of the main reasons. That, plus the fact that you always hogged most of the sheets-- especially after we just had terrific, mind-blowing sex."

Silence. I enjoyed leaving her speechless. It gave me a feeling of great triumph. Psychiatrists would love hearing that, but I didn't care.

"Ralph, how much did this person--this crime boss--tell you about Jackie?"

"Nothing."

"What were you two talking about?"

"He did the talking. I just sat there with a hood over my head and answered his questions."

"A *hood*?"

"You know, one of those cloth things--"

"I know what a hood is, thank you. Why would they want you to wear a hood?"

"He didn't want me to see him. Or know where I was."

"He didn't . . . hurt you, did he?"

"He just wanted to know why I was snooping around. Then he let me go."

"What about the unconscious thing?"

"He had to get me out of there without my seeing him."

"But you were wearing a hood."

"Those guys don't take any chances. They're kind of secretive."

"As well as kind of psychotic."

"Possibly."

"And totally crazy."

"A lot of them, I guess."

"And homicidal. And disgusting. And--"

"I get it, Phil."

"So you don't think he knows about Jackie?"

"Not really. But don't worry. I still have a few leads to work on."

"It's almost eight o'clock. She's been missing eight hours, now."

"Sounds about right."

"Don't you think you should call the police? This could be a kidnapping, you know."

"I don't think it is. Even so, a person isn't declared missing for twenty-four hours. And there's no evidence of foul play. Has her mother called you recently?"

"Her mother?"

"The woman who brought the little bundle of joy kicking and screaming into the unprotected paradise we call our civilized world."

"Why should she?"

"If this is a kidnapping, the parents should've been contacted long before now. Her mother would naturally call you to find out what happened at the hotel."

"I didn't even think of that. . ."

"Something like this would be handled much differently if the girl was underage. But since she's an adult. . ."

"I understand. But she's still missing. We should both consider ourselves lucky her mother hasn't called her daughter yet."

"The mother would've called the daughter long before now. If the girl was missing, the mother would've definitely called you to ask what happened."

"That's right. . ."

"And if the girl was kidnapped, her mother would've called her daughter's cell and found herself talking to the kidnappers. Don't you consider that strange?"

"Maybe the two women don't talk much. You know how college kids are. I know how I was."

"A mother and her daughter not talking much? Especially when they're coordinating a surprise birthday party for the father?"

"When you put it that way, it does sound odd. Whenever I was coordinating something, I walked around for three days with the phone glued to my ear. What do you think is happening, Ralph? This is getting stranger by the second."

"Give me a little more time."

"Do you think you can sort this out?"

"It's what I do. Why I get the big bucks."

"But this sounds so . . . so *weird*. . ."

"I'm pretty good at weird. Lots of experience. If you've seen some of my clients. . . Anyway, we have until tomorrow at noon, right?"

118

"The party's scheduled for two."

"Even better. I've got to hang up now."

A deep sigh. "Don't tell me you have company again."

"Just an idea."

"Tell me about it."

"Can't. Confidential."

"I understand. I don't like it, but--"

"You never have."

"I don't think I ever will."

"I'll call you."

"And Ralph?"

"Uh-huh?"

"*Please* be careful."

"Ah. You *do* still care."

"Of course I still care."

"That gives me a warm fuzzy."

"Please do me another favor."

"What's that?"

"Stop being silly."

"Me? Silly?"

"You are, you know," Mike said. "You really are."

"Don't agree with her."

"Who are you talking to, Ralph?" Phil asked.

"My conscience."

Chapter 10

Charlie-Joe's Bar & Grill sat in some woods at the end of a sandy path about fifty yards off Narcoossee Road.

Since I needed a strong drink, I decided to stop and check it out. A few minutes earlier, just as I turned off 192 to head north, Mike vanished again. Her sudden disappearance startled me, of course, but since I was still jumpy from my talk with Paseo, I actually welcomed the quiet time.

I pulled into the gravel lot. All four vehicles parked out front were mud-splattered pickups carrying dog cages, hay bales, and rolls of field fencing, indicating that Charlie-Joe's preferred the casual drinking crowd. I parked between two of the pickups. A sticker on the passenger door of the truck on my left said, *FORGET THE DOG, BEWARE OF ITS OWNER!* The message didn't help soothe my paranoia, but my overwhelming craving for a drink won out, pulling me inside.

The sign nailed to the center of the heavy wooden door said: *C'mon in, take a load off! We're waitin for ya!* The sign didn't exactly bring a smile to my face. When you've just been abducted at gunpoint, forced to wear a hood, slapped in the back of the head, then chloroformed and dumped, you're cynical of everything and everyone.

The large room, an eclectic mix of Western and rustic, smelled of leather, cheap aftershave, and cigarette smoke. Wagon wheels leaned against the paneled walls. Battered copper lanterns dangled from the thick wooden beams. Ceramic pots sat on the hearth of the stone fireplace. Dry-rotted saddles hung from posts. A pool table filled the opposite corner, where three large men in overalls and stained white tee shirts smacked balls, drank draft beer, and belched loudly, drowning out Tanya Tucker's suggestive cooing from the juke. Two sloppy-dressed gentlemen sat at the bar, chatting with the bartender, a portly middle-aged man with a shaved head. I took a small table in front of a window. I was too tired to climb a barstool. I was also too tired to engage in mindless conversation. I just wanted to relax.

A short, dumpy woman in loose jeans and an ill-fitting hunting shirt waddled over. Her nametag said *Hi! I'm Dee*. She was probably at least sixty and wore enough makeup to hide most of the wrinkles and blemishes. Her dark red wig probably went for $19.95 at J.C. Penny's Spring Sale. The large silver dream-catcher earrings made her huge, fleshy earlobes appear even larger. She didn't crack a smile or exude the vibes necessary to make me feel like a valued customer. She just listened to my order and waddled back to the bar.

Despite her laid-back appearance, she brought my drink within two minutes and placed it carefully on top of a cracked plastic coaster that said, "*Thanks for joinin' us!*" She was gone before I could thank her or tell her how ridiculous her wig looked. It was a blessing, though. I didn't want to be smacked so soon after being chloroformed.

I sipped my drink. It was strong. I put the glass back down, sat back, closed my eyes, and let the

121

whiskey warm up my limbs and soothe my joints. One or two more of these and I'd be back on the road to recovery. But I knew I shouldn't have more than one. I still had a job to do.

I opened my eyes. Mike sat in the chair facing me. She wore a cream-colored short-sleeve shirt with a turquoise shrug and her usual jewelry. I couldn't see her slacks or what she had on her feet. Somehow, that didn't matter. It was all an illusion, anyway. A delicious one, but still an illusion.

Our first embarrassing encounter in public had taken place just a few weeks ago, at Smilin' Susie's. This happened long before I realized Mike was dead, and I ended up looking like a mental case, sitting at a booth, talking to myself. Right now, I had no intention of looking like an idiot in front of a few half-drunk good-ol' boys, so I placed both elbows on the table and rested my chin in my hands to hide my mouth. The juke wasn't on very loud-- Garth Brooks had replaced Tanya with a ballad. I could speak softly without giving myself away.

"I may have found out a few things," Mike said.

"From who?"

"Trade secret."

"Where was this?"

"That's also a secret."

The oversized pool players shuffled over to the bar. They ordered three more drafts and leaned against the counter, talking to the guys on the bar stools about some double-jointed stripper named Mimi. Dee waddled over, saw that I still had whiskey in my glass, then returned to the bar.

"What did you find out?" I asked Mike.

"After you were taken back to St. Cloud, Smith drove north on Narcoossee Road, then turned onto Moss Park Road. He stopped at a secluded lakefront lot right on Marine Court."

Moss Park was a beautiful area. From what I'd heard, a lot of big shots owned lakefronts out there. "Those lots go for half a mill, easy," I said.

"Is that important?"

"It could be."

"Smith made a call from the car. He didn't use a name but we have this feeling he was talking to a woman."

"We?"

She nodded.

When a woman wants you to know something, she tells you. If she doesn't and you press her anyway, you're in for a very unhappy rodeo. I learned this long ago, from Phil. "How could you tell it was a woman?"

"Men puff up and grin a lot. Sound like Barry White. Act stupid."

"Define stupid."

She laughed. "Anyway, he mentioned money-- lots of it. He also mentioned moving more merchandise in the morning."

"You didn't see exactly where his place is?"

"He made a right on Marine from Nell, then I left him and came right back."

"How'd you get back?"

She smiled.

"I know. Another trade secret."

***

Moss Park Road runs east for several miles before it forks into Lake Mary Jane, a long, winding stretch leading to subdivisions separated by slender patches of woodlands left by the developers, possibly to remind the few who still cared that the area had once been rich woodland.

A pair of low-flying sand hill cranes missed the hood of the TransAm by inches. A quarter of a mile later, a trio of deer nonchalantly crossing the road forced me to an abrupt stop.

"Please don't hit them," Mike said. "They're so cute."

"If they'd cross at the posted *Deer Crossing* signs like they're supposed to, they wouldn't have to worry about being hit."

"Maybe they're not interested in road signs."

"Or maybe they can't read--like the illegals, or the latest generation of kids coming out of high school."

"By the way, what will you do when you find Smith?"

I didn't know how much snooping I could do while he was home, but once I found a residence, I could take it from there. I might be able to come back tomorrow for a better look. If Smith had kidnapped Jackie Frazier and was keeping her here, I'd have to find out for sure before giving it to the Feds, but OPD would have to be notified first, or Neil would never forgive me. "I have to find out if he's holding the girl."

"If he's kidnapped her for some sort of white slavery thing, he'd probably already have a buyer, and would move her fairly quickly, right?"

"That sounds reasonable, but since we don't know what's going on, I can't rule anything out yet."

"You won't try and rescue her by yourself, will you?"

"I'm not that kind of detective, baby."

"What kind are you?"

"The non-violent, non-confrontational kind."

Mike wrinkled her nose. "Really?"

"You sound skeptical. And you look like you've just smelled something rotten."

"Look how violent and confrontational you were on that case when we first met."

"That was only because every time I turned around, some moron was trying to kill me."

"Like the meeting with Paseo?"

"That wasn't actually a meeting."

"Whatever. But I think I can probably help you out here."

"It might be tricky. Smith has already seen the TransAm. This means I'm probably going to have to snoop around on foot."

"That could be a bummer. It's soft ground out there. There are probably all kinds of slimy critters."

"I really don't have much choice." Driving a classic car comes with its liabilities. The biggest one, of course, is that it sticks out like blinding neon.

I wanted to say hell with all this, drive back to civilization, and stop somewhere for a cheeseburger and fries. I also had to sample my mom's *biscotti*. I'd definitely have a couple in the morning with my coffee. Anyway, I really needed rest. My unscheduled drug nap had thrown my system off. The whiskey helped a little, but on an empty stomach, it had intensified the throbbing in my head. I wanted to call it a night. But until then, I had to find something that would tie in with the girl's disappearance. I didn't have much time. If I didn't find her before two o'clock tomorrow afternoon, Phil was going to be in serious trouble.

***

As we drew nearer to the lake, the homes grew larger and more luxurious.

The number of luxury cars and classy boats parked in carports and driveways also grew. Fences turned from galvanized aluminum to iron. Lawns and shrubbery gave evidence of professional care. Since Mike hadn't given me a street number, I was going to have to improvise. The darkness--along with the shrubbery and the trees separating the lots-- would conceal me but would also make my search more difficult.

As I coaxed the TransAm down the winding road, the distant thumping of music penetrated the warm night air. Farther down, Marine Court branched off into private roads leading to ritzy-looking buildings nestled among trees, flowers, and lush shrubbery. Spotlights lit up Spanish roofs, carports, gazebos, and verandas. In the background, the mirror-like surface of the lake reflected the coppery haze of the moon. The splashing of water and playful screams penetrated the night air. The thumping of music continued. Hopefully, Smith's Corvette would be parked outside. I also hoped I didn't see more than one red Corvette. So far, I'd seen only Mercedes, Porsches, BMWs, a Lexus, and half a dozen other expensive rides.

I veered around the bend. A large Spanish-style villa sitting amongst palmettos, palm trees, scrub oaks, and rich shrubbery came into view. A red convertible sat alongside another low-slung vehicle in the lighted carport on the west side of the house. I eased off the road and inched the TransAm into some bushes directly across the street, then doused my lights and grabbed my binoculars from the glove box.

The red Corvette, its Manta tag clearly visible, dozed peacefully. A Ferrari sat close beside it. Interesting. Unless Smith was just visiting, this setting suggested a major miracle for a man declaring $24,000 on his last income tax return.

With my lights still off, I pulled back onto the road and searched for a place to conceal the TransAm. A driveway farther down would suffice. The lights in the house at the end were restricted to the living room. Floodlights at each corner met in the center of the front yard. There was no sign of life. I sat and listened.

"What are we doing?" Mike whispered.

"Listening."

"For what?"

"Dogs."

"I don't hear any."

"Neither do I." I put the binoculars back, took out my penlight, slipped it in my pocket, and made sure I had my locksmith tools with me. Then I locked the doors and started the walk back.

Splashing sounds increased as we drew closer. The name on the black mailbox said: *VEGA*. The front yard was dimly-lit. The floods focused mainly on the paved drive. I slipped through the open gate, veered right, and ran across the front lawn. Once I reached the house, I ducked down beneath the shrubbery and moved toward the back.

The splashing grew louder. I peered around the corner. A large, kidney-shaped pool connected to an L-shaped patio that extended to a screened-in Florida room. Totally naked, a slim, light-haired man pushed himself out of the pool. Dripping wet, he padded over to the patio, where a drink tray sat on a round table beneath a green umbrella. He toweled off and draped it around his shoulders, picked up a glass, and drank. He put the empty glass back and picked up a bottle to replenish his drink. I was too far away to tell if it was Smith. He faced the house, which revealed his left side, but the towel obscured his neck. Even without the towel, his tattoo couldn't be seen at this distance.

"Want me to take a closer look?" Mike whispered.

"If you don't mind."

She was gone in a flash.

A woman's low, accented voice drifted lazily over to me. The man immediately straightened. A tall, slender woman in a flimsy black two-piece bikini came outside, carrying a drink. She was obviously not Jackie Frazier. She walked over, pushed her long black hair over her right shoulder, put her arms around him, and kissed him passionately. After the kiss, they finished their drinks and put them on the table. The man tossed his towel and, taking his girlfriend's hand, persuaded her to join him in the pool.

"It's him." Mike said when she came back.

"Can you do me one last favor while we're here?"

"You want me to sneak inside and look for the girl?"

"Actually, I wanted to ask you to sneak inside and look for the girl."

"Isn't that wonderful? We can read one another's minds."

"I'm getting a little misty-eyed myself. Now make it snappy, all right? I have a feeling there's a Neighborhood Watch out here somewhere."

"I'll be right back. Don't go anywhere." Before she left, she said, "Aren't you gonna tell me to be careful?"

I sighed.

She laughed. "Where's your sense of humor?"

"I left it in the car."

"Go find it before I get back, okay? You're taking all the fun out of this." Then she was gone.

***

Mike came back less than two minutes later. "She's not in there."

"Nowhere?"

"I looked everywhere. Every square inch of space. Not a sign of anyone else in the house."

I should've known. If Smith kidnapped the girl, he certainly wouldn't keep her here. "Well, it was worth a shot."

"What's next?"

"I don't know. But that girl's got to be somewhere."

My cell buzzed just as we were about to slip through the front gate. It was Phil.

"Your ex again?"

"Who else?" I clicked it on. "Phil, I can't talk right--"

"Good news," she said cheerfully. "I just heard from Ruth."

"Who?"

"Jack Frazier's wife."

I stopped walking. "What's going on?"

"Everything's fine."

"Fine?"

"I don't know what you did, but whatever it was, it worked."

"*What* worked?"

"I'm *so* relieved. I almost called the police, I was so nervous."

"Phil, what's going on? What are you talking about? This have anything to do with the daughter?"

"Apparently she's been in her hotel room all day. I guess we just had some sort of mix-up and were worrying over nothing."

"She's *fine*?" I couldn't get past that.

"Anyway, I started thinking about what you said earlier? About the two women not communicating? It just didn't make any sense, so I decided to do a little investigating on my own."

None of this was actually happening. It was my exhaustion taking its toll. That drink I had at Charlie-Jo's. That crap they'd stuck into my face. I was hallucinating. "Phil--"

130

She laughed. "I know how weird that sounds, but I couldn't help it. I was so worried, I called Ruth. I had a story worked out--you know, some alibi I could use as a reason why I was calling. But I didn't need to tell her anything. Before I could say much, she told me how she and Jackie had spent the afternoon on the phone, making sure the catering service had everything right, and that all the people who were invited were coming. Naturally, I was surprised, since I'd been so worried all day. Ruth said everything went perfectly. Jackie loves Florida and can't wait to visit the theme parks, and. . ."

I didn't hear the rest. I couldn't get past the idea that the girl was just fine and had been just peachy all afternoon. This was some kind of bad dream. I wanted to pinch myself. I also wanted to get drunk. I decided to get drunk first, then pinch myself.

"Ralph? You still there?"

"Still here."

"I'm really sorry for how things somehow got messed up. I hope you'll let me pay you for your time."

"Sure. No problem."

"Good. Just let me know how much and I'll cut you a check."

"Sure. No problem."

"Ralph? You *sure* you're okay?"

"Sure. No problem."

A pause. "Good. Well, thanks again. Good night. Get some rest. I'm sure you're tired. I know *I* am."

I clicked off and held the phone in my hand, glaring at it. I wanted to toss the damned thing.

131

"What's wrong?" Mike asked.

I decided not to toss the phone. I'd only have to buy another one, and I was mad enough as it was. I pocketed it, then marched down the drive in full view of the lights. I didn't care who saw me, or if there was a Neighborhood Watch. I crossed the road and went back to where I'd parked the TransAm.

"Ralph?"

I'd actually forgotten Mike was still with me. I'd forgotten a lot of things, but that was because I had only one thing on my mind. "I'm a schmuck."

"What's wrong?"

"I don't like being a schmuck."

"Ralph . . . can you please give me a little more information here?"

"The girl's just fine and dandy."

"The girl we've been looking for all day?"

"She's the one."

"Where is she?"

"Apparently she's been in her hotel room all day."

"The girl we've been looking for all day?"

"She's the one."

"The one with the tattoos and the jewelry and the attitude?"

"She's the one."

"Ralph, she hasn't been in her room all day. . ."

"You noticed that, too?"

"Of course I noticed. I've been with you most of the day."

"That's right. I've been with you, too."

"Then what's your ex talking about?"

"She doesn't know."

132

"Know what?"

"What's been going on."

"What *has* been going on?"

"I've got no idea. But I intend to find out."

PART TWO

The Brat Returns

Chapter 11

The next morning, after a shower, shave, and light breakfast of toast and coffee, I was already planning my day.

Once I found Jackie Frazier, I intended to ask what she was doing with Smith and why she wasn't in her room when I went looking for her. I'd ask why she'd conned her mother into thinking she'd been at the hotel all day, and why her suitcase wasn't in her room when I checked the second time. I'd ask who moved it. And why. And where she'd gone. And when she'd returned to her hotel room.

These were very simple questions. None of them mattered to anyone but me. No crime had been committed--at least, none I knew of. And since the girl had not been kidnapped or was in any immediate danger, I had no reason to see her again.

If I was smart, I'd say hell with it, drive to my office, and wait for a prospective client to walk in. But I'd been through a full day of hell and wanted to find out why. When someone goes out of their way to cause you trouble, your first instinct is to find out why. At least mine was, and I'd been going with my instinct for years. If the girl was involved in something illegal, I was not only going to find out, I was also going to bring her down.

By nine, the vast sea of glittering rooftops had turned the parking lot of the Presidential Resort into a blinding starburst.

I parked in a visitor's space between a blinding white Lexus and a glistening light-gray Lincoln Town Car, then followed the caravan of bright-eyed guests into the air-conditioned lobby. The main area hummed with activity. Guests crowded the front desk. Some stood in other people's way, talking to cell phones, while others followed the harried porters to the elevators.

The bar wasn't open yet. This saved me the bother of checking it out. I didn't think the girl would be there even if it was open. If she was awake, which was doubtful, she'd be getting ready for Daddy's surprise birthday bash.

The restaurant was chaotic with stressed-out waitresses and hungry, demanding guests. I went through the glass door and stopped a few feet in front of the cashier to survey the scene.

The cashier was short and slender, about twenty, with plain features and thick black hair. She wore a frilly white shirt with a green apron and black slacks. She smiled behind her podium. "Good morning, sir."

"Morning." I continued to scan the crowd behind her.

"Our special is--"

"Thanks. I ate at home."

Silence. She began to pout. I felt as if I'd just kicked a dog--a small one, with cute little ears and a big floppy tail. How can some people make you feel

135

guilty even though you haven't actually done anything to feel guilty about?

"You look very nice this morning," I said, hoping to bring her around.

She suddenly stopped pouting. Her smile showed two rows of tiny white teeth. "*Thank* you."

"Your white shirt . . . it brings out your . . . beautiful dark hair."

She blushed. I decided to finish scanning the room quickly. I didn't want to end up asking her out. Judging by her glazed expression, I had a feeling she might beat me to the punch if I didn't move away fast. You can always tell when a female hasn't been noticed or complimented in a while. The glazed eyes give them away.

Once I decided Jackie Frazier was nowhere in the room, I took the elevator up, went down the hall, and stood in front of the door marked 222. I pressed my ear against it, but heard nothing. Since I didn't have the tools to open a card-reading door, I'd have to knock or wait for another maid. Knocking was out of the question. You can't sneak into someone's room very well if you knock first. You also can't catch them off-guard--especially if the door is equipped with a peephole. Luckily, a maid was coming down the hall. Like her predecessors, she was short, thickset, dark-haired, and Latin.

"Excuse me," I whispered. "Could you please open this door? I left my key inside."

She stared at me, then at my clothes. I guess I didn't appear as sloppy as the other rich guests. I should've worn my sweatshirt, cutoffs, and flip-flops. She turned toward the door, stared at it, then went back to staring at me. Her large black eyes drifted down. A horny maid? Actually, she was staring at my pocket. I sighed in relief. I'd overestimated my charm, poise, and rugged good looks. I pulled a ten-spot out of my pocket and handed it to her. She quickly stuffed it down the front pocket of her apron, pulled out her master, and unlocked the door.

I thanked her with a smile, watched as she scurried away, then silently pushed open the door. Once again, it only took me seconds to realize the hotel suite was empty. The bed hadn't even been slept in.

My instincts were right. The girl *had* been lying to her mother.

***

I rode the elevator back down to the lobby and checked to make sure the bar hadn't opened yet.

The sign on their door said they opened at eleven. I gave the dark room a quick glance anyway--just in case Ms. Congeniality had bribed her way in. Then, dodging roving tourists, I found an armchair in front of a window in the carpeted area leading to the pool and tennis courts out back. While two slender young babes in skimpy two-pieces lounged under the bright haze of the morning sun, I dialed Phil's number. It took me three tries. For some reason, I suddenly found it difficult to concentrate.

Phil answered on the second ring. "How much do I owe you for yesterday?"

"I haven't given it much thought."

137

"Then why are you calling? I've got a meeting in fifteen minutes and--"

"This won't take long."

"Is it about yesterday?"

"Good guess."

Silence. She'd picked up on my dark tone. Phil knew me better than anyone else. "You had a very long, stressful day. I'll pay whatever you ask. It was stressful for me as well, although obviously not nearly as bad as what you dealt with. You *should* be paid for it."

"I agree. But that's not why I'm calling."

"Something's wrong, isn't it?"

"That call you made to the girl's mother. What exactly did she say about her daughter?"

"Just that she talked to her and everything was fine."

"Did she mention the girl's hotel room?"

"Why would she?"

"I don't think the girl's been there at all."

"What exactly does that mean?"

"Here's what I've got so far. I don't think she's been in her room since I dropped her off."

"Where would she stay if not in her hotel room?"

"You tell me."

"Maybe … maybe she went to stay with her mom."

"Then why didn't her mother call you?"

"Why would she? And why do you sound so . . . so upset?"

"You asked me to do a little favor. It *was* a little favor, too. Any kid with a car and a driver's license could've done it easily."

"Ralph, are you blaming me for--"

"You're absolutely blameless here. The mother isn't. I'm blaming her for not calling you and telling you about an obvious change in plans. And I'm blaming the girl for treating me like crap, then skipping out without a word, which resulted in all sorts of hell for me."

"How'd she treat you like crap?"

"Take my word for it. Their little bundle of joy is no joy."

"I . . . don't know what to say."

"Neither of us knew what we were getting into, apparently."

"And what is *that*?"

"I haven't found out yet."

"Ralph, if I thought for one moment this would have ended so badly--"

"Where's the party?"

"The Marriott, on Sand Lake Road."

"Why there?"

"Ruth knows someone working there who manages their catering."

"And it's still on for two o'clock this afternoon?"

"What are you planning to do?"

"I don't know yet."

"Ralph . . . this is important to me."

"I realize that."

I heard her sigh. "Several important clients will be there, as well as Jack Frazier."

139

"I figured as much."

"How did you know *that*?"

"Frazier's rich. The rich always seem to have more friends than regular people."

"What are you talking about?"

"Haven't you ever seen those shows where the rich are having a bash and call it a "small, cozy affair" because they've only invited fifty or so of their "closest" friends?"

"I believe so. . ."

"How many close friends do *you* have?"

"Point taken."

"Is this going to be small and cozy?"

"There shouldn't be more than twenty people there."

"Then it shouldn't take me long to find out something."

"Ralph, I'm afraid you're going to do something that will probably embarrass me, the Frazier's, the guests, the caterers, and probably the entire hotel management staff as well."

"Wow. I sound impressive."

"I'm serious, now."

"All I wanted to do this morning was ask the girl a few questions. But when I got here and found her suite empty, I knew something just wasn't right. I've got to find out, one way or the other. The party is my only lead."

"Why do you need to confront her? She's apparently fine. And judging by what her mother said, she's very happy and excited to be here."

"I'm really pleased to hear *that*."

"So why must you stir the pot?"

"Two reasons. First of all, I'm a die-hard pot-stirrer."

"You'll have to do better."

"How's this? I was almost killed because of her."

"You . . . didn't tell me that."

"I told you I was talking to a crime boss, didn't I?"

"You didn't tell me you were almost *killed*. . ."

"Things like that usually happen when you're brought in to see a crime boss to answer questions about why you were on his turf, asking questions. Crime bosses don't like questions. They're paranoid. And they employ people to take care of that."

"Why weren't you . . . I mean, why didn't he--"

"My story checked out."

"And *that* was why he didn't . . . kill you?"

"If anything I said *hadn't* checked out, we wouldn't be having this conversation. You'd be deciding if you were going to my funeral."

"You don't think I'd attend your funeral?"

"Sometimes I wonder."

"Don't. I'll certainly be there."

"I'm *so* relieved. But don't sound too eager."

"As long as you don't do anything to make it happen very soon."

"When I have to deal with people who point guns at me, force me to wear a hood, then take me to their leader, who happens to be a crime boss, I can't guarantee anything."

"*Now* I see why you're so upset."

141

"Trust me. I won't do anything to screw up your party."

"I don't want you to do anything that'll screw *you* up, either. . ."

"Like I said, something's going on and I've got to find out what it is."

"Will I see you at the hotel?"

"I'll probably stay in the shadows and look for the girl, then leave as soon as I finish asking my questions. Just how long that takes is up to her."

"I just hope you don't find out anything incriminating."

"That's the bad thing about asking questions. You have no control over the answers."

***

After talking to Phil, I had a quick bite at one of the fast-food places on Sand Lake Road, then arrived at the Marriott at just a few minutes before one.

The parking lot was packed. I found a vacant place in the back, a hundred yards or so from the rear entrance of the main building. I hiked past the rows of bungalows and a cluttered sea of vehicles winking at me in the afternoon sunlight. Straight ahead, heavy streams of traffic roared by. A block west, clogged traffic choked the intersection of Sand Lake and International Drive.

The hotel buzzed with activity. Delivery trucks blocked the loading dock entrances. White and blue uniforms scurried in and out of the building, lugging boxes and pushing carts piled high with food items and cases of champagne and wines. A big guy in a dark jacket drove a forklift stacked with palettes of canned food through the huge square doorway. White-uniformed drivers tossed white sacks into the laundry trucks parked at the other end of the building.

As I drew closer, the parked vehicles grew shinier and more expensive. Stretch limos lined the shaded porte-cochere. Off to the side, another limo sat sandwiched between a shiny gray Rolls and a shimmering black Bentley. On the other side of the Bentley, a red Corvette sat, watching me. It was Manta.

I stopped in my tracks. A quick scan didn't spot Smith amongst the workers or the tourists roaming the lot, searching for their vehicles. No one resembled the man I'd seen last night in Moss Park, but with so many people milling about, it was difficult to get a good look at anyone. Once you've been kidnapped and taken somewhere at gunpoint, everyone looks like a bad guy.

A short, slender guy in a baggy white shirt, black pants, and patent-leather black shoes marched hurriedly in my direction. He probably came from one of the delivery trucks and was able to get close because of the rows of vehicles separating us. He looked like he was just out of high school. His left forearm and hand were covered with a white towel draped across it. The towel was engraved with the hotel's monogrammed gold *M*. It made him look like a misplaced waiter.

"Is this your car, sir?" he asked with a smile.

The short black hairs on the back of my neck bristled. He didn't appear to be a parking attendant. He stopped about three feet away--about a foot

143

inside my comfort zone. As a precaution, I stepped back. "Do I look like I can actually *afford* one of these rides?"

"This area is reserved for guests." He took another step forward. "Are you a guest, sir?"

Why would he want to know if I'm a guest? If he was a delivery man, he should be delivering things. If he was a parking attendant or valet service guy, he should be asking for my ticket. I took another step backward. "Who wants to know?"

"Are you on someone's guest list, sir?" Another step forward.

"You sure do ask a lot of questions." I stepped back again. "You look like a waiter. Shouldn't you be waiting on someone? Preferably inside the building?"

He moved forward again. "Is there some reason why you're checking out this car, sir?"

The hair on my neck bristled even more. Delivery men don't care about stuff like this. Neither do parking attendants. But I didn't appreciate how he kept invading my personal space. And I certainly didn't like that towel draped across his forearm. I shrugged. "I love Vettes. Always have. Can't help it."

"Where are you parked, sir?"

That certainly was a strange question. But I decided to keep playing along. I pointed toward the back. "My TransAm's parked about--"

"I suggest we return to your car, sir."

"Pardon me?"

"Please, sir . . ." With the thumb and index finger of his right hand, he pinched the front portion of the towel and carefully lifted it about two inches, exposing his left hand.

The snub-nosed barrel of an automatic pistol stared ominously at me.

145

Chapter 12

As I started up the ignition, my thoughts, as usual, centered on the Beretta lying snugly in the console, inches from my right elbow.

So close, yet so unobtainable...

Then I focused on the kid sitting beside me, pointing the gun at my side. His gun looked like an old model Walther--probably a 9-millimeter. He'd dropped his towel onto his lap--which made the small compact enormous and frightening. Its barrel, only about a foot away, did not waver.

Kidnapped twice in two days. It was unbelievable. If I were superstitious, I'd think twice the next time Phil asked me for a favor. But since I was a professional, top-notch detective with a cold, calculating mind, I knew better. The blame, in this case, rested on Miss Congeniality's shoulders.

"Where to?" I decided on the casual approach, as I'd done with Junior the day before. Casual can keep you from freaking in some cases. When you've got an automatic weapon pointed at your side, you need all the help you can get.

"I'll let you know when we get there." His smile had vanished. The only thing emanating from his small gray eyes was excitement.

Having dealt with armed psychos before, I didn't consider excitement a good thing right now.

"What? No *sir*, this time?"

"Just drive and maybe we won't have to worry about getting blood on your upholstery."

"We sure wouldn't want that." This kid obviously liked crime dramas with witty dialogue. I pulled up to the Sand Lake Road exit. "East?"

"You're good."

"I also read minds and know my ABC's." I pulled out and we joined the flow. "Let me guess. You're not really an employee of the Marriott, are you?"

"Just keep driving."

This boy was just as uncooperative as Junior. But at least he spoke better English.

"I hope you realize you're going to make me miss the party."

"Life's a bitch sometimes."

"Original. Maybe I'll write that down somewhere."

No response. Where the hell were these punks coming from nowadays? Didn't they have a sense of humor? Manners? Conversational skills?

"Have you heard the one about the guy who walks into a bar carrying a live baby alligator?"

"Nope."

"See, this guy walks into a bar--"

"Don't care to, either."

"It's funny."

"Not in the mood."

"Then put your gun down. It's obviously taking the humor out of all this. Guns have their uses, but let's face it, they're not really good for lightening the mood--"

"Nice try."

"I'm back," Mike said, smiling from the back seat.

147

"I was beginning to worry if I'd ever see you again." Suddenly Psycho Boy and his gun didn't frighten me as much.

"You're really funny," he said flatly.

"I've been told that once or twice before."

"He's younger than the other kid," Mike said.

"He looks like he's on a high school field trip."

"Talking to yourself?"

"I do that a lot."

"Get any answers?"

I couldn't help grinning. "You'd be surprised."

"Figures."

"Good disguise," I told Mike.

"Apparently it worked," she said.

"It's simple, and lets me carry my gun around in public," the kid said. "Nobody even notices me."

"How nice for you and your gun."

"We're pleased you're okay with it."

"I'll bet your boss doesn't have a problem with it, either."

No reply.

"I don't know who he works for," Mike said. "I saw him talking to Alan Smith earlier, at the Marriott. I didn't have a chance to listen in, so we're going to have to play this by ear."

Not much to go on, but it didn't surprise me.

"I saw the daughter as well," Mike said, and I perked up. "She was in the bar, but I didn't see her talking to Smith. She had one drink, then left to join her mother and the other guests."

Things were getting even more complicated. We crept up to the light at South Orange Blossom Trail.

"Get in the left lane and head north," my companion said.

"Bad section up there," I said. "Tittie bars, drugs. Lots of weird, spaced-out people roaming around."

"Don't worry, I'll keep you safe."

Something bothered me about this kid. "How old are you? You look like you're still in high school."

"Old enough to carry this gun."

"*That* sure is a load off my mind. I was worried we'll be stopped and you'll be hauled in for unlawful--"

"Shuddup."

"I've been working on my ectoplasm," Mike said.

"Your *what*?"

"The stuff that lets you see me."

Junior frowned. "Talking to yourself again, buddy?"

"I do it when I'm nervous."

"Why're you nervous?"

"Don't be funny."

"Just drive."

"And for the record, I'm not your buddy."

"Ouch."

I tried a long shot. "You wouldn't want to stop somewhere, would you?"

"For what?"

"Coffee? Doughnuts? The Police Station, maybe?"

"Why the Police Station?"

"I'd like to report a crime."

149

"Crime?"

"You know--something unlawful."

"Such as?"

"Kidnapping. Unauthorized use of a firearm. Despite what you said, I don't think you're old enough to--"

"You're quite a character, buddy."

"The name's Deacon. And I'm *not* your buddy."

He shook his head. "Yeah, you're weird, all right. Just don't try and con me."

"How can I do that? You're the one with the gun."

"Shuddup and drive."

"I can't. I always go on when I'm nervous."

"Do your best."

"No offense," Mike said, "but you do go on sometimes."

"Really?"

She nodded.

"I didn't realize--"

"Didn't realize what?" the kid asked.

"That I go on so much."

"Why d'ya think I keep saying shuddup?"

"Um, you really suck at small talk?"

"A real comedian."

We approached the intersection of South Orange Blossom and Colonial and stopped at the red light. "Now what?" I asked.

"Keep heading north."

"The light's red."

"Wait till it's green, *then* head north, asshole."

"The name's Deacon."

"Try to find out more about him," Mike said.

"So they're paying you for kidnapping me? Pointing that gun? Threatening me? Refusing to participate in relaxing conversation?"

"Just keep driving."

I didn't like this area at all. Chop-shops were scattered out this way as well as prostitution rings and dump spots for bodies. I didn't care too much about the chop-shops or prostitution, but the dumping thing had me spooked. We followed the flow and went straight several miles, past a trashy trailer park, a couple of trashy nightclubs, and a large two-story garage with the sign *BILL'S BODY SHOP* nailed to the front door. Behind it, an auto graveyard littered the sloped countryside as far as the eye could see.

"Turn here."

I eased off the main drag and took the car down the short sandy path, stopping in front of the garage. The place looked abandoned.

An abandoned *garage* during the lunch hour? This was looking worse and worse.

"Go around toward the back."

"Why?" I was getting even more uneasy. "It's not that the TransAm doesn't need a tune-up, but I didn't bring my checkbook--"

The gun jabbed my ribs. I did as ordered. We went down a narrow sandy path leading to a couple of battered aluminum sheds and one of those huge car-crusher things they used in *Goldfinger*. I grew more uneasy by the second.

"What was that thing you said you were working on?" I sincerely hoped Mike had a real showstopper up her sleeve.

"I'll let you know in just a minute," the kid said.

"I wasn't talking to you."

"Yeah, a real comic, all right. Stop the car."

"Was it something I said?"

"Get out, then go around and open the trunk."

"The *trunk*?"

"That's what I said."

"Why the trunk?"

"You'll soon see." The smile returned.

"I think he wants to put you and your car in that crusher thing," Mike said.

"He must be crazy," I told her.

"Stop the shit and do what I said, asshole."

"Deacon. And if you think I'm gonna climb into my own trunk and let you put my car in that--"

The gun pointed directly at my face. "You heard me, goddammit. Now do what I said, or--*what the fuck*?" He twisted his face toward the back seat and slammed his back against the door. The gun was still pointed in my direction but had turned a little toward his left. His jaw dropped; his face turned white. The gun shook.

"What's wrong?" I asked. "Seen a ghost?"

He gawked at me, then at the back seat. He tried talking but could only manage a series of raspy throat sounds. The gun lowered a couple of inches.

"How's that?" Mike asked, grinning.

"How's what?"

"Like I just told you, I've been working on my ectoplasm."

It registered immediately. "You mean . . . he can actually *see* you?"

She nodded. My passenger continued to gasp.

"Mike? Meet the kid with the gun. The kid with the gun? Meet Mike. She's my dead buddy. The one I've been talking to."

The gun dropped to the floor. The kid twisted around, groping for the door handle. I picked up the Walther and slammed the barrel into the back of his skull. He gasped, slumping like a rag doll into my lap.

"How sweet," Mike said.

I pushed him away. His forehead whacked the door frame. He slid back down, his head slapping my console.

"Damn. Now I've got to haul him in."

"You didn't say anything about my new trick." Mike was pouting.

"Sorry, but I was a little distracted. I had to do something with Psycho Kid, here. I hope you understand."

"So what did you think of my new trick?"

Women were *so* insecure. Even the dead ones. "That *was* cool. Really and truly. I'm pleased. And impressed."

"I just saved your life, you know."

"I noticed. I was here, too, remember?"

"Then why the mad face?"

"I have stuff to do, but now I've got to waste the afternoon taking this jerk to OPD and explaining what happened."

"You can't just leave him here?"

"I'm the *good* guy, remember?"

"Can't you take a break from that?"

I couldn't leave this kid here. It wasn't that I felt sorry for the moron--I just didn't want him coming to and finding me later on. Besides, there were too many psychos wandering the streets already. "You know, sometimes being honest and doing the right thing really pisses me off."

Chapter 13

Neil Haversack was obviously having a rough day.

His eyes were bloodshot, and his customary close-shaven cheeks bore splotches of blond stubble. I figured he had either constipation or a nagging hangover. Or maybe one of his bosses was giving him a rough time. I knew better than ask. Asking someone why he looks like shit can be dangerous. Besides, you don't want to piss off someone who could possibly help you in an ongoing investigation.

Mike decided not to come in with me. She preferred being with Flo and her new circle of dead friends. I couldn't blame her. Being in a place filled with cops can make anyone nauseous--alive or dead.

Neil handed me a cup of boiling battery acid, then sat down and slurped some from his own cup. I stared at mine and was instantly reminded once again why I never wanted to be a cop. For starters, you've got to have a cast-iron stomach. "I see your good luck streak is still holding up," he said flatly.

Neil was obviously still somewhat confused about things suddenly going my way since Mike had come into my life. I could sympathize. It must be terrible, hearing things that don't make sense and not being able to evaluate them. But I couldn't tell him a dead babe had come back to life to help me in my work. Cops weren't real big on the afterlife. "You don't sound too pleased about it," I told him.

"Sorry. Every time I try a cartwheel, the change falls out of my pockets and I have to spend the next twenty minutes gathering it all up."

"Carry around less change."

"Then I wouldn't be able to fatten up the kitty so I can enjoy all this wonderful coffee. Now . . . where were we?"

"My good luck streak."

"That would be a fair assessment, wouldn't it?"

"If you ignore my superior brain skills and razor-sharp reflexes, I guess so." I'd put the Styrofoam cup carefully on the edge of the metal desk. I blew on it, hoping to scatter the thick cloud of steam that would let me see Neil's face behind the desk. But it didn't. I slid it very gently, about a foot to my left. I didn't want to spill any of it on my hand and carry around a horrible welt for the rest of my life.

"Tell me about that punk you just brought in. Just someone you picked up along the way? Or is there something else you'd like to share?"

"Actually, there's quite a bit."

"I was afraid of that. Want to tell me once again how you took that gun from him? I don't think I heard it quite right the first time."

"Why should it confuse you? I'm a trained professional."

"From what you said, a kid barely twenty held a gun on you from about two feet away. You not only managed to take it from him, you also hit him over the head with it, then brought him in all by yourself."

"You *did* hear everything right the first time. I'm impressed."

"It was actually very intriguing and entertaining. I'd just like to hear it from the beginning again." Neil knew how to ask an innocent question and make it blow up right in your face if something didn't quite make sense.

"Like I said, he forced me into my car at the Marriott when I was on my way inside."

"So please tell me how you snatched a loaded gun away from him. I might want to write it all down and submit it as possible training material for the Police Academy."

I wasn't in the mood to think something up, so I decided to give him the truth for a change. Sometimes the truth works. Especially when it's embellished with a white lie or two. "The boy was obviously tripping. Claimed he saw something in my back seat, then tried clawing his way out of my car. He went berserk and dropped his gun. I picked it up, rapped him on the back of the head with it, then brought him here. The rest--as they say--is history."

"I guess that sounds possible."

"I thought so, too."

"Why don't I believe it, then?"

"You haven't been sleeping well? You haven't been laid in a month or so? Your blood pressure's up?"

Neil drank more coffee. "I just lack an imagination for incredible stories. When they've finished questioning that kid, I sincerely hope some of what he says actually jibes with your yarn."

"We've been such good friends. How can you doubt anything I say?"

"You're not serious."

"When have I ever been not serious?"

"I believe all this is the result of that blow to the head you took outside Kelsey's a few weeks ago. You haven't been the same since. Or maybe your biorhythm's been on the upswing. Whatever happened, you now seem to have developed at least eight senses. No matter how deep a hole you get yourself into, you always manage to climb out of it. I'm still trying to digest why Raguzzo quit putting out hits on you."

"What are you saying? You don't like it that Raguzzo hasn't had me killed? Or do you think I'm on his payroll?"

"Raguzzo wouldn't use someone like you. He wouldn't put up with your stupid quips."

"You don't, either. . ."

"But I wouldn't have you killed just to get you to stop."

"You've got principles. I like that."

"I'm a cop. We're not allowed to put out hits."

"I'm so glad you've explained your principles so well."

"So . . . any idea who that kid is?"

"None whatsoever."

"He just walked up to you at the Marriott, showed you his gun, forced you into your car, and made you drive up the Trail into Chop-Shop City?"

"This is my second abduction in two days."

"You're kidding me, right?"

After I told him about my interesting drive to Kissimmee the day before, Neil got up and went back to the coffee pot sitting on the metal table in front of the tinted window. "Good deal. You've met Paseo. Got a description we can use?"

I carefully sipped a tiny drop of the boiling coffee. It tasted awful and scalded the tip of my tongue. I put the cup back down and forced myself not to dump it in Neil's trashcan. Neil was sensitive for a cop. "He's got a heavy Hispanic accent and a deep voice."

"How helpful. Got anything else?"

"It's hard to see much when you're wearing a hood."

"Ah, the hood deal..." He brought the coffee back and sat. "Paseo sounds pretty bright. You have no idea where you were, who he was, or what he looks like. Just a voice and a name--which could belong to anyone."

"What have you got on him so far?"

"Nothing under that name." Neil put down his coffee and attacked the keyboard. "Nothing from DEA. The FBI doesn't even mention the name. If a man named Paseo had any connection whatsoever with drugs coming up from Cuba, Mexico, or Jamaica, the Feds would have a file on him. That name must be phony. Either that or he's clean, but judging by how expertly he handled you, he obviously knows how to stay out of the spotlight."

"He said I'm all right as long as I stay a zit. Once I become a carbuncle, that's the ballgame."

"Good thing you didn't stay with him a minute or so longer."

"You're all heart."

"One of my less desirable qualities."

"Anything in there about escort services?"

He sighed. "Central Florida's the escort service capital of the east. Between this place and Miami, we can wipe out Vegas."

"Nothing about a new service starting up, say, within the last few weeks?"

"Impossible to keep track of. Most operate strictly through referrals and word of mouth. The only ones we can actually nail are the morons stupid enough to advertise in the Yellow Pages, or online. The outfits working the high profiles are off-limits because they handle people we can't mess with. But I personally don't think you're on the right track. Paseo isn't the one you should be worried about."

"Why do you say that?"

"He let you live."

"Besides that?"

"Isn't that enough?"

"You're right. Smith's the bad one here."

"You're not even sure of that."

"My gut tells me I'm on the right track."

"I just don't see why you're pursuing this. Let it go."

"I don't like being kidnapped every time I snoop around."

"Stop snooping around."

"I'm a professional snoop. Professional snoops snoop around."

"That doesn't mean sticking your nose in something when you don't have to."

"It's personal now."

160

Neil huffed. "How'd I know you'd say that?"

"Um . . . you know a smart man when you see one?"

"No offense, but I'm still looking."

"Wouldn't you be interested in what's going on if this kept happening to you?"

"I'd be too busy getting on with my life before someone decided to bring it to an abrupt end."

"Doesn't it bother you that bad guys are out there and you don't even know who they are?"

He had some coffee. "Do I look bothered?"

"You *should* be bothered. You're a cop. It's your job to nail bad guys."

"The only thing bothering me right now is a certain private eye who's gonna end up dead because he's too stubborn to walk away from a possible fatal situation."

"I can't walk away."

"Sure you can. It's very simple. Turn around and just keep putting one foot in front of the other."

"I will after I find Smith."

"Don't say I didn't warn you."

"He's into something. I can smell it."

"You can't even find him."

"His boys keep finding *me*."

"You don't even know they're his."

"Who else would do this?"

Neil chuckled. "I can think of a few dozen others you've crossed paths with who might try to give you a bad day."

"You're a real ego booster."

"All you know about Smith is that he has no address of his own, works at a small business in town, and declared twenty-four grand last year."

"And drives a really sweet luxury car worth three times that."

"It could be a gift."

"What about that estate in Moss Park?"

"You said he was with a chick. She probably owns the place."

"She's Hispanic."

"Your point? Most of the Hispanics I know have more money than I do."

"That isn't fair."

Neil groaned. "Deacon, tell me you haven't been with a chick who has more money than you and I'll get down on my knees right now and personally kiss your ass."

"As inviting as that sounds. . ."

"You know I'm right. Admit it."

I hated when Neil made so much sense. I also hated it when he made me feel stupid. "I have a sort of contact in St. Cloud, says Smith scares him to death."

"This sort of contact. What's he do?"

"He works at Walmart."

"What else?"

"We don't exactly pal around."

"How'd you two meet?"

I shifted uneasily in my chair.

Neil chuckled. "This must be some story."

"He was . . . picking my pocket."

"Terrific. A pickpocket. Pillar of the community."

"He's getting his act together."

"Does he drink?"

"What does that have to do with--"

Neil sat forward. "Here it is in a nutshell. Your friend--a former pickpocket, now a Walmart employee who drinks--says Smith scares him, and you automatically think it's because Smith is a bad ass--not because this friend of yours might be a nutcase."

"He also said he's seen Smith with some strong-arm guys who work at the strip joints. He doesn't know if Smith is a strong-arm, but he's seen him driving around a large Hispanic. The word on the street says the big guy's from Colombia. He's sure it's Paseo. He says Paseo's into protection and has been targeting the pawnshops. Does any of this sound like something a nutcase would say?"

"How many nutcases do you know, Deacon?"

"Counting myself? Quite a few."

"Any of them make sense? Talk coherently? Act fairly normal?"

"Excluding myself? Just about all of them." I was beginning to think I'd wasted my time coming here. Maybe I should have done what Mike suggested and left Psycho Boy lying on the ground near the compacter. Being professional and conscientious comes with too damned many liabilities.

Neil went back to his keyboard. "Smith graduated from Rollins College eight years ago and earned a degree in Computer Science. That's all we've got on him."

"What have you got on Jack Frazier?"

163

"He's a high-profiler involved in land acquisitions."

"He buys land?"

"He's a glorified go-between arranging deals for buyers and developers. He's a lawyer who knows contracts, acquisitions, and buyouts like the back of his hand."

"I was hoping he wasn't legit."

"Deacon, you need to see less bad in people. Read Norman Vincent Peale. Go to church occasionally. Watch *The Bells of St. Mary's,* or maybe *The Yearling*. Get inspired."

"You serious, Neil?"

He shrugged. "So where are you with Frazier's daughter?"

"I wish I knew."

"You still haven't seen her since you dropped her off?"

"Every time I try finding her, I end up staring down the wrong end of a gun barrel."

"You want to give me a description of the first guy who kidnapped you?"

"Later, after I find out a little more."

"Sounds like this first kid might be working for Paseo. Or whoever Paseo is."

"I'm pretty sure Smith's working for the same outfit."

"Like I keep saying, nailing Smith's gonna be tough. What about this kid we've got in Holding?"

"He popped up when I got close to Smith's Vette."

"I'll let you know what we find out. Can't promise anything, though. Ever seen *The Stone Killer*?"

"Damned straight. Charles Bronson. One of my heroes."

"This kid has that same blank, stupid look as the killers in the movie."

"He was smiling when he showed me his gun."

"Stone killers only seem to come alive when they're killing somebody, or about to. Like sharks, when they bite down on something. These boys get high, but most don't use anything when they're working. You *sure* he was tripping?"

"Why else would he glance at my back seat and freak out?"

"What were you carrying in your back seat?"

I shrugged. "A Wendy's wrapper, some old napkins, and a large supply of fresh, exhaust-laden Florida air."

"Maybe he's schizoid and took in airplane glue once too often. But like I said, they're usually sober during a job."

"Conscientious. I'm touched."

"They just don't want anything interfering with the thrill."

"He's awfully young to be a killer."

"They're recruiting them younger nowadays. Kids don't aim for college like they used to. Four years of study for a job starting at fifty grand takes too damned long. You can buy a stolen gun on the street for a couple of hundred, work for the Mob, and make a grand a hit."

"When you put it that way. . . ."

"Economy's not helping. People are angrier. Makes 'em want to kill more."

"The other guy's only a year or two older than this boy."

"I'll bet he's used that gun of his a few times already."

"You should've seen him pull it out. I didn't see it and I was watching him at the time."

Neil frowned. "I hate to say this again, Deacon."

"I know. I'm in over my head."

Chapter 14

The afternoon heat had turned the black interior of the TransAm into a steamy hotbox.

I immediately rolled down the windows and cursed myself once again for not having the compressor replaced.

Phil buzzed me. "How'd everything go at the Marriott? I didn't see you there at all."

"That's probably because I never made it."

"You decided not to go?"

"It was decided for me."

A pause. "I know I'm going to regret asking, but oh well, here goes. What happened?"

"You probably won't believe me."

"Ralph, I don't think I've ever gotten a simple answer from you since we've known one another. I strongly suspect what you're about to tell me won't surprise me."

"I was kidnapped."

"You were also unconscious. We've already been through this, haven't we?"

"This happened at the Marriott."

She gasped. "*Again*?"

"I liked it so much the first time--"

"Ralph, *please* be serious for once and tell me what happened."

After I told her, she said, "Ralph, what on earth am I going to do with you?"

"You had fifteen years to figure that out but blew it by walking out on me. From that day on, I haven't been myself."

"Don't blame *me* for your physiological changes. Besides, I don't believe there *are* any. Despite what you put yourself through in that horrible profession, you're still you, Ralph. You'll always be you."

"That sounds like a catchy song title."

"This is nothing to joke about."

"You can say that again. It's really no fun, having someone point a gun at your face. . ."

"I knew it was a mistake to get you involved in this."

"Why'd you ask, then?"

"I told you. No one else was available."

"Is that the only reason?"

"What else would there be?"

"The way this looks, it could be the perfect way of getting rid of your ex."

"Stop that. I don't like that kind of talk, Ralph. Not even in jest."

One giant flaw in Phil's character was that she never liked joking about certain things. Having me killed was one of them. "You still there?" I asked.

"You didn't . . . you don't suspect *I'd* be involved in . . . in whatever is going on, do you?"

"Of course not."

"Are you *sure* you don't suspect me of anything?"

"Other than walking out on me and doing ridiculously well in business, your slate's clean."

"But I *am* sorry I got you involved in something that has turned out to be so . . . *dangerous*. It was just a simple errand. But it's gotten so *risky*. . ."

"I'm not wild about risks, either."

"Taking risks is part of your job. You've told me that a hundred times."

"That doesn't mean I actually like it."

"Then why in heaven's name do you do it?"

"The high pay. The glamour. The interesting people I meet. The flexible hours. I even get to carry a gun. Once in a while I even get kidnapped, knocked unconscious--"

"I knew I shouldn't have asked. Let's please get back to this latest kidnapping. You don't think Jack's daughter is involved in any of this, do you?"

"I have no idea."

"You think . . . she actually *might* be?"

"Anything's possible."

"I saw her at the party. She was all over her father."

"Um, that could be taken several different ways. Please explain."

"Sometimes you can be such a . . . a--"

"Man?"

"I was looking for something else--more of the four-legged, canine variety. But that'll do as well. Anyway, Jackie sat next to her father at the table. She kissed him, hugged him several times, even said a few tender words for a toast. It was very touching."

"I know *I'm* tearing up, and I wasn't even there. . ."

"I can't believe she'd be involved in something . . . something illegal. Or dangerous."

"I can."

"But if you'd seen her at the party--"

"I picked her up, remember?"

"I meant--"

"I even talked to her. I tried to, anyway."

"She wouldn't talk to you?"

"I got on her bad side when she took one look at my TransAm and refused to get in."

"What's wrong with your TransAm? Apart from being old? And polluting the air? And horribly noisy?"

"It's a *classic*." I hated when she talked badly about my car. She could be so snobbish at times. Phil's idea of the perfect car was something that cost eighty grand, had GPS, luxurious seats, and was so quiet, you didn't know when it was running. "The girl was expecting a first-class ride in a stretch limo."

"Is that what upset her?"

"What really got her off was what came later on."

"What did you do, Ralph?"

"I wouldn't let her smoke her joint in my car."

"She . . . does marijuana?"

"You sound surprised."

"I guess I wasn't thinking along those lines. . ."

"I wasn't in the mood to get pulled over. From then on, we weren't exactly what you'd call buds."

"You'd expect someone with her breeding to have more finesse."

Mike appeared beside me in the seat. A grim look covered her face.

"Something wrong?" I asked.

She nodded.

"Ralph? Did you just ask me what's--"

"Can you tell me now?" I asked Mike. "Or should I hang up?"

"You'd better hang up. This won't make your day."

"Ralph, are you talking to someone?"

"Got to go," I told Phil.

"Ralph . . . is everything . . . all right?"

"Just fine. But I've got to go."

"Are you sure? I mean, if there's someone pointing a gun at you again, just give me a clue and I'll call the police."

"A clue?"

"For heaven's sake, Ralph, just call me Honey or something, then sign off. I'll know you're in danger and--"

"I'd rather call you Baby. Or Sexy Legs. How's that?"

"Does that mean . . . are you . . . is there someone--"

"I just wanted to call you Sexy Legs again." I pocketed the cell. "What's so bad?" I asked Mike.

"I found Alan Smith."

"Where is he?"

"Lying on the concrete floor in an industrial warehouse."

***

Just an hour earlier, Mike had found Smith back in Moss Park with the sultry Latina chick.

Smith then got into his Vette, drove directly to the Florida Exotic Travel office on Semoran Boulevard, asked the receptionist about someone named Petie, then sat down and waited. While he waited, the receptionist returned to her telephone.

171

Each time a line blinked red, she clicked on it, whispered a time and a place, then forwarded the call. She handled nearly a dozen calls in the two minutes Smith waited.

Smith's cell phone finally buzzed. He said, "Yeah, right away," hung up, left the office, got back in the Vette, went down the road, made a left, and drove to the rear of the complex, where a row of a dozen warehouses sat in front of the woods bordering the property. He parked beside a tan Ford pickup outside the third warehouse from the end, got out of the car, and went inside.

Mike followed him in.

The area was pitch-black, but Smith obviously knew his way around. He went to the back, to a cluster of cubicles. As soon as he slipped into the first one, the door slammed shut behind him. Two figures had been waiting for him. Both were tall, broad-shouldered, dark-featured, and around twenty-five. One of them quickly stepped behind Smith and wrapped a muscular forearm around Smith's neck. Smith struggled for a couple of seconds, but the other man was very strong and easily broke Smith's neck. The other man grabbed Smith's ankles and the two of them dragged him back out, leaving him in the middle of the floor in the main area. Then they got into the Ford pickup and drove away.

"Where?" I asked Mike.

"North Semoran Limousine Service. It's about a mile or so north of Colonial. They went in through the back."

"You didn't lose them, did you?"

"How can I lose anyone? I'm dead. But I didn't accomplish anything. They looked like all the other guys there."

"Guys?"

"You know. People who aren't females--"

"No offense, but smartass is *my* specialty."

"Sorry."

"Who were these other guys?"

"Well, since the back lot was filled with limos, and they were dressed like drivers, I assumed they were limo drivers."

This was beginning to wreak. "You mean with the tux? Hat? Spit-shined shoes? Blank expression?"

"They were also fairly dark, tall, and around twenty-five."

"Hispanic?"

"Some, I guess. Not all."

"Could you ID these two if you saw them again?"

"Like I said, they all looked similar--as if they were all from the same family."

"How many did you see?"

"A dozen or so."

"And what did they do next?"

"They went into a locker room, and I followed them in."

"You didn't mind being in a men's locker room?"

She sighed. "Have you already forgotten where *we* met?"

"A men's room, in one of the worst bars in Orlando."

"You remembered. How lovely."

"I'm getting a little misty-eyed myself. So what happened then?"

"Don't you remember? You were suckered from behind and dumped--"

"Here, dammit. In the men's locker room." She was being a butthole again. One of these days, I was going to have to talk to her about that. "I know what happened at Kelsey's. I was there, too, remember?"

"Sorry. I guess I was still being nostalgic. Anyway, they got dressed, went back out to the main area, and waited around. When their cells went off, they hurried outside and got into their limos."

"So you obviously couldn't follow them, right?"

"I thought I'd better get back so I could tell you what happened. Did I screw up?"

"Nope."

"Would you tell me if I did?"

"How long have you known me now?"

"That was kind of stupid, wasn't it?"

Chapter 15

South Orlando Business Center, a sprawling mass of office complexes, warehouses, and storage buildings, encompasses thirty acres of commercial real estate off South Semoran Boulevard, just a few miles north of Orlando International Airport. More than a hundred businesses keep their records and supplies in the one-story modular buildings sitting on small slabs just twenty feet from one another.

According to Neil Haversack, Florida Exotic Travel is so new that it has not yet been listed in Central Florida's Business Section, the Yellow Pages, or even the Net. After Mike and I left the OPD Building and headed east, I called Neil and asked him to find what he could about the company. It took him several minutes to find it on one of his sites. "Why do you want to know about this place?" he asked. "Does it have anything to do with Smith or the Frazier girl?"

"Smith was spotted going inside this building."

"How did you know to even go there?"

"An anonymous call." I shouldn't have said anything that would prompt Neil to ask more questions. Luckily, I knew how to talk my way out of just about anything.

"And just who else knows you're working on this?"

"If I told you, I wouldn't be able to follow through on these leads."

"These leads of yours are scaring the hell out of me."

"No need to fear, my good man. I've got my eyes wide open."

"That scares me worst of all."

Twenty minutes later, Mike and I reached the Business Center complex and found the place without much trouble. The air-conditioning in the dark office, set about thirty degrees cooler than the outside heat, made me shiver as soon as we went inside. Mike didn't shiver--apparently you don't feel heat or cold when you're dead. Right now, I envied her.

My eyes needed several seconds to adjust to the darkness. When I could see again, I surveyed my surroundings. The room, about fifteen by fifteen, smelled of Lemon Pledge and *Tabu*. Photos of vacation spots all over the world covered the paneled wall behind us. Pamphlets and brochures lay in neat rows on the long folding table. A door to our left was marked *Office*, the one directly to its right, *Bathroom*. A modular desk faced us straight ahead. Two folding chairs faced the desk. To our right, a large color shot of Bermuda hung on the wall beside the front door.

The girl sitting at the desk was about twenty, slender, and reeked of *Tabu*.

"She's not very nice," Mike said.

"I'll warm her up," I whispered.

"You'll need a blowtorch."

"My charm won't work?"

Mike sighed. "I'd hold out for the blowtorch."

The girl was smartly dressed, her tan showing clearly beneath her open-collared, cream-colored blouse. She also wore a turquoise shrug--possibly to

176

keep her from shivering while she handled her calls. Judging by the disapproving way she glanced at me, I figured Mike was right. This girl was probably one of those many shallow, arrogant young females everyone sees these days. She and Jackie Frazier were definitely cut from the same mold.

She was whispering into the tiny black rod extending a few inches from her thick pouty lips. Her dark-brown hair was so thick, you could hardly see the headset protruding from her right ear. It told me why she was whispering. Handling a call, apparently. Only the wire trickling down the front of her blouse was visible. She touched a button on her switchboard just as I walked up to her desk.

"I'm looking for a certain limo driver." I flashed my irresistible baby browns and gave her my patented little-boy grin. I knew this was supposed to be a travel agency, but I had to try and trip her up, so I figured my best bet was to play clueless and naïve.

"We don't employ drivers," she said flatly. Apparently she had no tolerance for the little-boy type, either, possibly because she liked her men more prosperous. I'm sure the sweat-stains darkening my shirt didn't help my cause.

"You can't help me at all?"

"We're a *travel* agency. You know what a *travel* agency is?"

I tried a long shot. "Travel stuff?"

"We make arrangements for vacation bookings, plane flights, cruises--"

"Say I wanted a limo."

"You'd have to contact a *limo* service."

177

"You don't do that?"

"We're a *travel agency*." Her large dark eyes blazed briefly. Mike might have been on the right track with her blowtorch idea.

"Any idea where I can find a good limo service?"

"We only do vacation bookings."

"How about plane flights?"

"Those, too."

"You aren't affiliated with any specific limo service?"

"No."

"How about the one on North Semoran?"

A sigh. "That would be a no as well."

"Say I wanted to make arrangements for--"

"One moment." She pressed a button, turned her head, and spoke very softly into her headset. An instant later, she pressed another button on her switchboard. I couldn't tell which button it was.

Mike had drifted over and stood right behind her. "She just pressed *HOLD*."

The receptionist turned back to me. "You were saying?"

"That could be a customer," I said.

She didn't reply.

"Don't you think you should be handling that?"

"I'll get to them just as soon as you leave."

"Don't want to chit-chat?"

"I'm working."

"When are you off? I could come back and--"

"I don't date guys I don't know. And you're too old for me. Besides, I don't like you."

178

I gave her one of my irresistible grins. "Don't sugar-coat it, now. I'll understand if they won't let you date prospective customers."

"You're boring. And not the least bit amusing."

"I understand. Dating prospective customers can be awkward. And distracting. You could mess up bookings, forget what you're doing--"

"Have a nice day." She'd said it coldly while glancing at the door. Her expression clearly said, *Don't slam it on your way out*.

I wasn't quite ready to let her see the last of me. "A friend of mine told me he works here. He's a limo driver."

A groan. "We don't--"

"You don't use limo drivers. I know, but I saw his car parked out there. Maybe an hour ago? A red Corvette convertible. His tag says Manta. Maybe you know him. His name is Alan Smith."

Her blank expression did not waver, although she blinked at my mention of the Corvette. This was one cold bitch. I could see why she was picked for this gig.

"I take it you don't know the man."

She shook her head.

"Thanks for your help."

She turned back to her headset.

I wanted to ask her if she wore it during sex. "Do you have that on when you're--"

"Hush," Mike said.

"How do you know what--"

"I can see it in your eyes."

Having your own guardian angel is almost like having your mother peeking over your shoulder all

179

the time. I went outside and got back in the TransAm.

"She's calling someone now." Mike appeared beside me a few moments later, as I started up the ignition.

"She sure is busy in there."

"This time, she's *making* a call. She mentioned you."

"I never knew a travel agency that does business that way."

"What way is that?"

"The ones I know of go into their computers and pull up flights and fares. The conversations are much longer than just a few seconds. Customers ask questions about where they're going. And how long it'll take. And isn't there a cheaper and better way to fly? Besides, all the agencies I know of use limo services, or at least have access to them."

"Her monitor was set on screensaver. It showed a really pretty panoramic view of the Rocky Mountains."

"That makes it kind of difficult to look up flights and fares."

"I honestly don't think it's a genuine travel agency."

"It's obviously a front. All Miss Personality does is transfer calls."

"What sort of calls?"

"Going by the amount of oration she did, I'd say she sets up appointments. And handles redirects."

"Regardless of what she told you, I think they're connected to that limo place."

"You're getting there," I said. "Soon you'll be able to branch out on your own, grasshopper. Open your own place. Nail a shingle to the door."

"I don't think I'd do very well."

"Why not?"

"I can't nail anything. And people don't pay much attention to you when you're dead."

"I do."

"You're different."

"I didn't think you noticed."

***

My nerves shook as I parked beside a tan Honda Accord in the paved drive facing the warehouse.

My nerves always shake when I know I'm about to get into trouble. In this case, sticking my nose in what was probably a murder definitely qualified as getting into trouble. I kept hearing Neil's voice, telling me to back off, to walk away. But I had to find out what was going on. When you're a private eye, it's what you do, and what people pay you to do. No one was paying me in this case, but if a murder had taken place, I had no choice but look into it.

I've always been funny about things like that.

The red Vette was nowhere in sight. If Smith was inside, the car would still be out front. Since it wasn't, I assumed that whoever did away with Smith would have moved the car. And if there were two of them, as Mike said, one might be ditching it right now. That meant the other--possibly the owner of the Honda--remained in the building.

"You're going in with me, right?" I asked Mike.

"Why would you even ask such a thing?"

"This could be very dangerous, you know."

"I'm dead, remember?"

"It's kind of hard to forget."

"I'm so glad. But you're the one who should be careful. You're still alive."

"I've got to find out if this is a homicide. If it is, I have to report it. That's how the system works."

"Don't forget the call that receptionist just made."

"You didn't by any chance hear any of that, did you?"

"She didn't say much. Just that some weird older guy had just come in, asking about Alan Smith, then hit on her."

"*Me*? *Older*? I'm not even *forty*."

Mike just sighed.

"And I didn't hit on her, I was just being pleasant. And funny--regardless of what she said."

"It sounded like you were hitting on her."

"Why do so many women think you're hitting on them when you're just being pleasant and funny?"

"I'll let you figure that out. Right now, I'd think about other things. For example, the person she just called. I have a feeling it might be the same man who murdered Alan Smith."

"That sounds reasonable. But before I do anything else, I need to go in there and check that out."

182

"Do you think that's wise? I just told you the person she was talking to might be inside this building, waiting for you."

"Your point?"

She sighed. "Can't you just call this in and have the police handle it? They have guns and everything."

"The police need probable cause, then a search warrant to get them inside the building."

"I didn't think of that."

I killed the ignition. "You can save me a lot of trouble, you know."

"You mean by slipping inside and making sure Alan Smith is still lying there?"

"Gee, I wish *I'd* thought of that."

"Be back in a sec." She disappeared. I pulled out my cell and punched in Neil's number. Just seconds later, Mike reappeared beside me in the seat. Her expression told me the worst.

"Let me guess. He's gone?"

A nod.

"What else is wrong?"

"Someone's inside, like we figured."

"What's up?" Neil asked. "I'm a little busy right now."

"Someone with a gun," Mike said. "He was sitting behind a desk in one of the cubicles, watching your car pull up. He's got a monitor hooked up beside his laptop. He was screwing a silencer onto his gun when I went in there. He's on his way outside, through the back."

I fired up the TransAm, backed out, and hurried down the block. I glanced in my rearview. The tan Honda was backing out of its spot.

"I think this is gonna turn into a chase," I told Mike.

Neil said, "Deacon? You there?"

"Hi, Neil. How you doing?"

"Don't pull that crap on me. You called no more than half an hour ago and asked me about that travel company--"

"Florida Exotic Travel? Yeah. I found it. Thanks."

"What the hell do you mean, *thanks*? Didn't you also tell me you saw Smith there?"

I pulled out into heavy Semoran traffic. Making full use of the TransAm's powerful 400 cubic-inch engine, I floored it, heading north.

"Deacon?"

"What I said was, I *thought* Smith was here."

"He's following," Mike said, watching the rear.

"I know. I see him."

"Who're you talking to, Deacon?"

"Myself."

"Sounds about right. Are you *sure* that's what you said? You *thought* Smith was there? What the hell's going on? You sound even crazier than normal."

We roared through the light at Semoran and Pershing just as it turned red. Several vehicles behind us, the Honda sat in traffic, growing smaller in my rearview mirror. I crept up to the next intersection and turned left with the light, covering a

184

full block before turning right. I went up two streets, then cut back to Semoran a couple of miles north.

"Deacon? What the hell are you up to?"

"I have this sneaking suspicion Florida Exotic Travel isn't really a travel agency."

"So you're calling to tell me something I'd already figured out?"

"I thought you might want to check it out."

"We're too damned busy as it is. Besides, I need a valid reason to send someone out there. Have you forgotten police procedure? What have they done?"

"They seem . . . shady."

"What?"

"The receptionist takes calls and redirects them. She didn't even smile at me. When a woman doesn't smile at me

--especially when I'm being my most charming self--I get suspicious. She wasn't even using her monitor, for God's sake. What kind of travel agency runs its business like that?"

"Let me get this straight. You want me to send a couple of uniforms to a travel agency because the receptionist didn't *smile* at you?"

"And because she acts shady."

"How the hell does someone *act shady*?"

"You know. Never smiles. Frowns a lot. Gives you that look."

"Deacon, don't call me again unless you're in a more professional frame of mind." He hung up.

I pocketed the cell. The light changed. We turned left with the rest of the flow, heading north.

"Where to now?" Mike asked.

185

"The limo place—where else?"

186

Chapter 16

I parked in the front lot of a strip mall one street north of North Semoran Limousine Service, in a vacant space beside a couple of green dumpsters at the corner. From here, I could keep an eye on things, and the TransAm couldn't easily be seen from the main highway.

The mall was just like the one my office sat in on Orange Avenue. Just a few stores, but instead of a Chinese restaurant and tee shirt place, this one provided a real estate agency, pet store, and takeout Mexican food. Like most strip malls, this one also boasted a liquor store.

It was close to suppertime. Since I missed lunch, I was hungry. I rarely eat Mexican food; it gives me the gazz and makes my stomach moan and gurgle for hours. But I couldn't be choosy. I'd better eat something to hold me over. I couldn't depend on Mike to drift on over there and order something for me. For one thing, she wouldn't be able to hold on to the money. And she'd probably do something ghostlike and freak out whoever manned the takeout window.

I jogged over, bought a non-threatening cheese burrito from an Asian kid with a nose ring and tatts covering his neck, then made a quick stop at the liquor store for a pint of Jack Daniel's before going back to the car. As I'd expected, Mike gave me some grief about the whiskey. She was dead, but she was also female. I'd never known a female yet who hadn't given me grief about something. "You shouldn't drink right now," she said. "You have to stay sharp and alert."

"I've needed a good belt the last couple of hours. I'll have food in my stomach, so I'll be okay."

"You're not an alcoholic, are you?"

I bit into the burrito. It was hot and tangy. The melted cheese scalded my tongue and lower lip. A quick belt from the bottle took away some of the sting. "I haven't thought about it much."

"If you need help, I'll have to drag you to those AA meetings. I don't think I'd like that--all those sad people sitting in a group, shaking and chewing their fingernails. I'd probably cry."

"That sure would be entertaining--the two of us sitting in a room full of drunks, you crying, me yelling at you for making me go there. They'll probably call for the guys in white coats to haul my ass right out of there."

"Then don't make me want to drag you to those meetings."

My phone buzzed. I sincerely hoped it wasn't Phil. I was right, but the display didn't exactly make my day. "Hi, Mom."

"Ralphie, did you get the *biscotti* I sent?"

"Sure did. And don't call me Ralphie."

"How were they?"

"Just great. You've always did bake the best *biscotti* in the civilized world."

"I'm glad you like them. It's not like they're fresh, though. You'll have to--"

"I know. Listen, Mom. . ."

"You're busy."

"I really am. But the *biscotti* hit the spot. I can't wait to have more when I get back home."

"You didn't eat them all, then?"

"Mom . . . you sent me a five-pound loaf."

"You could always eat a dozen without getting up from the table."

"I was a *kid*."

"You still eat, don't you? And you need to eat more. Last time you were here, you looked so *thin*. . ."

"I weigh a hundred and sixty-five pounds, Mom. . ."

"I don't care what the stupid scale says. You need to eat more. If you'd have good home-cooked food once in a while. . ."

"I know. But I can't eat that much anymore."

"You need to eat a *little* more."

"Mom. . ."

"Maybe you *did* eat too much when you were little. You always tended to overdo it, like your dad. Last time you ate *gnocchi's*, you ate so much, you had the gas."

"I remember. I was there."

"You also used to eat a whole pizza at one time, too."

"For my birthday. When I was a kid."

"I'm glad you're pacing yourself now that . . . now that you're--"

"Old?"

"You're not *old*, Ralphie. You're a young man."

"I'm almost forty. And don't call me Ralphie."

"Listen . . . I know you're busy, so I'll leave you be. Just promise you'll--"

"I'll be coming down soon."

"You promise?"

"Yes, Mom."

"Uncle Nicky's still waiting for you to--"

"I know."

"And stay away from the fast foods."

I bit into my burrito. "I will."

"What are you eating now?"

"A *biscotti*."

"It doesn't sound crunchy, Ralphie. Are you dunking it? You know not to dunk it so much, right? It gets all soggy and--"

"I know, Mom. And don't call me Ralphie."

"Call me once in a while."

"I will." I pocketed the cell and had another shot of Jack's.

"Your mom sounds nice," Mike said.

"Yeah."

"Why are you wearing your mad face?"

I shrugged. "She always calls at the wrong times."

"We need to visit her."

"We?"

"You don't want me meeting her?"

"You're not serious."

"You're not ashamed of me, are you?"

Sometimes I wondered about my dead buddy. "That's not exactly the issue here. . .."

"But you really need to see her."

"I know."

190

"I'm talking from experience. I should've visited my parents when I had the chance, but I never got to. By the time I decided to take a trip up north, it was too late."

I didn't speak. It's hard to reply to something like that--even when the person saying it is dead. You want to fix things, but you can't fix what has already happened, and it makes you feel helpless.

"I'll probably take a trip down there as soon as I wrap this one up." I figured that might make her feel better.

"Good. You should stay in touch with her."

"You act like I'm not long for this world."

"You more than anyone should know anything can happen."

"I'm careful. Besides, I've got you looking out for me."

"I can't predict what'll go wrong, you know. All I can do is warn you about certain things to help the situation shift more in your favor."

"You're doing a pretty good job so far."

"Even so, I can't predict what the bad guys will do."

"I do have to take certain risks."

"Don't forget, you've been kidnapped twice in the last two days."

"Thanks *so* much for remembering."

"Remember it the next time you're tempted to do something stupid."

"Define stupid."

"You know. Say you're following someone, and he. . ." She suddenly stopped and glanced down at herself. "Uh-oh. . ."

191

Her legs and hips had disappeared into the upholstery.

My pulse hammered. "What's happening? It looks like you're melting."

Her torso faded. "My ectoplasm. Used . . . it . . . up. . ." Her voice sounded very far away. Then she was gone.

"Mike?"

No reply. Once again, I was alone.

Just then, something crunched the gravel loudly beside me. A harsh rap on my door. I turned. A huge square fist slammed into my jaw. Everything went black.

***

When I opened my eyes, I realized I was lying in the back seat of the TransAm again.

A wave of grogginess, a surge of stabbing heat, and a strong sense of *déjà vu* overwhelmed me. My head and jaw throbbed heavily, but at least I wasn't wearing a hood. For some reason, that fact alone made the situation less awful.

It was nighttime, obviously. I brought up my arm and squinted at my watch, but it was too dark. A streetlamp sent down some yellow haziness toward my right. I tilted the watch until its face glinted in the light. 7:35. I forced myself up. More dizziness. *Relax. Fight the throbbing and focus.*

My TransAm was parked at the far end of a large, half-filled parking lot. About fifty yards straight ahead, a brightly-lit shopping center faced me. A green dumpster sat just a couple of spaces from the TransAm. Trash had been strewn all around it. The sour stench was overpowering on this

192

warm, muggy night. This area looked like the Trail, not far from the strip club district.

I pushed myself forward and propped my chin on the top of the front seat. Nothing dangled from the ignition.

The realization hit me hard. I was left here for a reason. Now I knew I had to get out of here. Fighting wooziness, I opened the front door and got in behind the wheel. I always keep a spare key fastened by a small ring to the dash behind the glove box, as well as in a secret compartment in my wallet and under the rubber mat beneath the driver's seat. When you've got a classic car, you spend a little money to have extra keys made. Dealers will take weeks--perhaps months--to find a replacement and charge you a small fortune for their time and your aggravation. I slid the mat a little to the left and shoved my hand underneath, until my fingertips found it. Exhausted by this minor effort, I sat back and let the heavy pounding in my swollen jaw subside.

My bottle lay on the seat beside the half-eaten burrito. The sight of the bottle made me want to leap for joy. The sight of the burrito made me want to puke. I picked up the burrito and tossed it out the window, onto the scattered pile in front of the dumpster. Being a model citizen, I never litter, but in this case it was justified. I decided not to pick up the bottle for a much-needed slug. Later, perhaps, when I was in less of a predicament.

Suddenly curious, I opened the console. My Beretta lay there, snug in its Uncle Mike's holster. Whoever brought me here either didn't care about the gun or wanted me to be found with it. I tried putting together a few possibles, but my groggy condition didn't tolerate much concentration at the moment.

"I can't leave you for a minute, can I?" Mike asked.

I stiffened at the sound of her voice. Ignoring the dizziness, I gawked at her, but saw no sign of her. "Where *were--are*--you?"

"Gathering up my reserves. I still can't make myself visible. Not yet, anyway. Guess I overdid it before."

"As soon as you disappeared, all hell broke loose."

"This isn't a very good place for you to be right now."

I looked around again. Still no one. "What are you talking about?"

"We need to move."

"I'm trying to figure out why I was left here like this."

"You want my opinion? Or would you like to wait and see what happens when the police show up?"

"The police?"

"They're on their way here now."

"Mike, cut the riddles. I'm not in the mood."

"Okay. There's a body lying in your trunk."

***

Less than a mile later, as we headed north, two cop cars whizzed past us, their lights penetrating the night.

194

"I'm glad you weren't unconscious longer." Mike spun around in the seat and watched them zip by. "Two more minutes and they'd be back there, arresting you."

"That's one way of getting me out of the way." Despite the fog in my head, everything had cleared up. "Knocking me out, driving me there, taking my keys, then calling the cops."

"They probably said they saw someone dumping a body, then hung up."

"Now I know why they took my keys."

"How'd you start the car?"

"I keep a bunch of spares lying around." I eased to a stop at the light, sat back, and let my nerves settle down.

"I should be really angry with you," Mike said.

"Why?"

"Look at you."

I glanced in the mirror. Even in the darkness my swollen, discolored left cheek stuck out. "I look like a chipmunk."

"Does it hurt much?"

"Only when I breathe."

"I told you to be careful. . ."

"I didn't have the chance. As soon as you melted into the upholstery, someone slapped me in the face with an engine block."

"Well, now we've got to find a way of helping you out of this."

The light changed. "I'm going to try giving them the truth and see what happens."

"The police are after you. You have a body in your trunk."

195

"Your point?"

"My point is this. You have a body in your trunk."

"You already said that."

"But listen . . . the body is dead, and it's in your trunk. Even the dumbest cop in the world will consider you the most likely suspect."

"That's why I'm gonna try the truth."

"You honestly think that'll work?"

"I don't have any other option."

"But you have a body in your trunk."

Mike was hot and I loved her. But like all hot women, she could be a pain in the ass. "Will you *please* stop mentioning that?"

"It's the truth."

"It's really irritating. And it bothers me."

"What? The fact that I keep saying it? Or that you've got a body in your trunk?"

"Yeah. . ."

"I'll quit saying it, then. But you need to do something about it, and fast."

"I have a friend in the Department."

"Can he help you with this?"

"He's not much of a friend if he can't."

"You're just going to drive to the Police Station and tell them you've got a body in your trunk?"

"My only other option is getting rid of it-- which I believe is a felony. And if anyone sees me doing it, I'm toast."

"I guess bringing it in won't be so bad."

"Neil will help me out, I'm sure."

"They won't find your fingerprints on the body, so maybe you'll be okay."

196

"They'll find my prints in the trunk, though. But it's my car, so they'll expect that. They'll just print everything and use their computer to delete my DNA out of the equation. The right technician can work this up in no time. But I really wish I knew what was happening here."

"I was there when they were discussing what to do about you. I was gathering up my ectoplasm, but I could still hear them. That guy Pete called them and told them what to do with you."

"What was their plan?"

"Frame you so you won't be able to do your job anymore."

"Smart. They get rid of me without actually killing me and get rid of someone they don't need any more."

"Makes sense. Especially since you're obviously irritating them."

"I'm glad *some* of this makes sense."

"Why are you irritating them?" she asked.

"It's my job, and I do it well."

"I mean, why do they consider your questions about the girl so threatening? I thought this was just an errand for your ex-wife."

"It obviously turned into something else."

"You think Paseo had them put the body in your trunk?"

"I don't think so. If he considers me important enough to get me out of the way, he would've just had me killed. Criminals only frame people they're afraid to kill, like politicians, journalists, and high-ranking cops, or Feds. I'm a nobody. No, this was done by someone else."

"So that's your plan? Just walk into OPD and hand over the body?"

"That's it. Simple, yet effective."

"You're sure about this?"

"I'm not sure about anything right now. I'm just too tired and hurt too much to concentrate on anything else." Then I took out my cell and called Neil.

Chapter 17

Neil stood beside me on the front steps of the OPD Building, watching the frenzied activity around my car.

Mike had vanished less than two minutes earlier, just as I'd pulled up to the curb. She hadn't liked the fierce expressions of the cops storming the front steps. "They look scary," she'd said.

"Cops are always upset," I'd said. "It's their job to be. And they're even worse when you bring them work."

"Things'll probably go better for you if I'm not around to distract you."

"That might not be a bad idea. You *are* very distracting, you know."

"Thank you."

The M.E., half the Forensics Department, and nearly a dozen uniforms swarmed like killer bees around the open trunk, taking pictures, dusting, sniffing--having a great time. Neil hadn't said much when I'd called him. His abruptness made it sound like I'd interrupted him doing something important. I didn't think he was about to have sex with his wife; he'd told me last year Nancy had started going through the changes and no longer wanted to be bothered. That lasted about eight months. However, he'd recently mentioned that even nowadays she "found herself in a frisky mood" once a month, if he was lucky. I figured I'd interrupted him during Extreme Fighting, or one of those Sports Illustrated swimsuit specials.

Once the pictures were taken and the hands and nails on the body bagged and sealed, two medical men carefully removed it from the trunk, laid it in a body bag, and zipped it up. Once the gurney was hauled away, two more Forensics guys closed in on the trunk and snapped away, then scurried past us. One uniform came over and asked me for my gun. He was wearing a disposable glove.

"It's in the console," I told him. He opened the driver's door and reached inside. As he bent over, his gut sagged down to the seat and his large ass provided a suitable target for the heel of my shoe. I wanted to mention it to Neil to lighten the moment but decided against it. I was more concerned why they wanted my Beretta. I didn't want to give it to them, but when a cop asks for your weapon, you don't have much choice.

The cop straightened. He gripped the Beretta, Uncle Mike's holster and all, in his left hand, then hurried past us and went inside the building.

"What was *that* all about?" I asked.

"We'll see in about fifteen minutes."

"I can hardly stand the suspense."

"Force yourself." Neil kept shifting his weight from one foot to the other, as an elephant does when it's chained up. Neil wore his civvies and looked like he'd dressed hurriedly. His shirt wasn't tucked in and half the buttons were unbuttoned. His eyes were blood-shot. Maybe he and Nancy *were* having sex. I decided to keep the jokes to a minimum. It's hard to joke around with a guy you'd just pulled away from his monthly piece of ass.

"When do you think I'll get my car back?" I asked.

"That's the least of your worries."

My jaw still throbbed. "I need an aspirin. Got any on you?"

He stared at my face as if just noticing it--not a good practice for someone who has to be observant for a living. "You look like shit. Who belted you?"

"One of my newer acquaintances."

Neil sighed. "Deacon, you need to start making better friends."

"I also need my car--"

"You bring in a stiff and all you care about is your goddamned *car*?"

"It *is* a classic, you know. I hope these guys don't mess anything up."

"Will ya stop with the damned *car*? You just brought in a *body*."

"I had nothing better to do, so I thought I'd find a body, mosey on in--"

"Deacon, stop being a dickhead. It's late and we're all tired."

"I'll try. But I'm sorry about the call. I figured I *had* to let you know about this."

"Actually, it's the smartest thing you've done in a long time. That is, unless you're the reason the guy's dead."

"*I* didn't make this happen."

"I sincerely hope so."

"You know I don't lie about stuff like this."

"I *thought* I did. Lately, I'm not so sure."

"I don't kill people--not even bad guys."

"I just hope the body you brought in was bad."

"I couldn't very well ask him, could I? You can't get many answers from a corpse. And if he *could* talk, he wouldn't tell me if he was bad, would he? If he was good, that would be something else. But why would he be lying in my trunk if he was good?"

"Deacon, will you *please* stop acting like a dickhead? Just for five seconds?"

"I can't help some of my reasoning comes out the wrong way."

"Next time you decide to *regale* us with your reasoning, clean it up a little before presenting it, okay?"

"I'll try."

"Now . . . I've got to find some way to explain this to my Captain without him wanting to pull both our heads off and stick them on the wall in his study."

My cell buzzed. I pulled it out of my pocket. "What's happening now?" Phil asked.

"This really isn't a good time, Phil."

Neil scowled. "Is that who I *think* it is?"

"Where are you?" Phil asked.

"OPD."

"What are you doing *there*?"

"I just brought in a body."

"A *what*?"

"A corpse. A stiff. You know . . . someone who's no longer breathing."

"Deacon, cut that call short. You need to be available. Totally."

"What *happened*, Ralph?"

"Well, it's like this. . ."

202

"I *said*, cut it *short*. We have to talk. *Now*."

"I'll just--"

"Now. Right now."

"Phil, I really have to go. My cop friend here has been salivating--"

"Frothing at the mouth," Neil said.

"Did you hear that?"

"Not really," Phil said. "I hear a lot of static."

"Probably the traffic. The clubs are just down the--"

"*Deacon. . .*"

"I have a feeling I'd better call later," Phil said.

"I'll call *you*." I pocketed my cell.

"Start talking, Deacon. And don't leave anything out."

"This might take a while."

"I'm not going anywhere. You haven't given me any choice. You just brought in a body."

"I know. I was here when it happened."

"That means we're both gonna be here a while. So you'd better make this visit as pleasant as possible--for *all* of us."

"Is that even possible?"

"Try telling us what happened. And do it professionally--*without* the smartass quips."

"I'll tell you what happened. That's no problem."

"You telling me there's gonna be a problem?"

"Only if you don't believe me."

Neil rubbed a large palm over his reddish brush cut. "The eternal optimist inside me is telling me you had no idea a body was in your trunk. At least I'm *hoping* you didn't."

"I didn't."

"Then why'd you bring it in?"

"I don't want it in my trunk anymore."

Neil stared at me, scowling again. It wasn't pretty. Neil wasn't a good-looking guy. He cleaned up okay when he shaved, put on his uniform, and forced himself to look pleasant. But with a scowl and messy clothes, he didn't present a picture suitable for posting on an online dating site.

"Inside." Then he turned his back and pushed open the glass door.

My head and jaw throbbed as I followed him inside.

***

Neil closed his office door and walked right over to the coffeepot.

The coffee smelled strong and had reached the shade of black you'd associate with burnt motor oil. Neil poured a cup and added a little sugar. He pointed to the stack of cups on the table. I shook my head. With the pounding in my jaw and the throbbing in my head, I'd put my body through enough torment. He came back to his desk and sat. "Start from the beginning. And don't take too long. I already put in a long day and was about to crack open up a can of Bud when you called."

"Sorry." I knew how much Neil enjoyed his beer. "Actually, I wouldn't have burdened any of you guys with this at all, but--"

"You just brought in a body. I'm sure you're already aware of this, but let me mention it anyway. Bringing in a body happens to be a crime--

especially when the body was murdered. We don't like it one bit. And it irritates the lab people."

"Really? I'd think they'd appreciate the gesture."

"They don't appreciate someone bringing work to them. The taxpayers wouldn't like it, either. They're more comfortable with the status quo. Makes 'em feel that maybe their tax dollars are actually at work. Also, it's more convenient for the lab people. They can dust for prints, check out the premises for clues, and use what technology they need to help them determine what happened. It gets them out of the office." Neil had a sip of the horrible coffee and frowned. "But when a body is brought in by a *citizen*--"

"I'm not a citizen, I'm a private eye."

"Actually, you're both."

"But--"

"When a body is brought in, *period*, the process starts out messy and goes south from there. All we've got are the prints on the body. So start from the beginning. And forget the smartass. You should've left it outside, anyway."

"You already know about Florida Exotic Travel."

"You said it might be a front."

"I think it's a fancy disguise for a new escort service."

"And how'd you come up with that?"

"Like I told you before, it's not run like a travel agency."

"That's right. The receptionist didn't smile at you."

205

"She did redirects. Nothing else. She wasn't even using her monitor--or her vocal chords. And as soon as I left, I went to the rear of the complex to check out one of their warehouses when a guy with a gun came out through the back and tried sneaking up on me."

"How'd you know *that*?"

"Know what?"

"A guy with a gun came out through the back."

"I . . . saw his reflection."

"You'd better be careful," Mike said somewhere behind me.

Instinctively I turned.

"Something wrong?" Neil asked.

"Just a slight twitch. This swollen jaw makes me do that."

"Probably jarred one of the nerve centers in your neck, as well."

"It felt like my head spun around like the Beetlejuice guy."

"Tell me how you saw this guy's reflection. And while you're at it, I wouldn't mind hearing why you decided to check out that warehouse."

"I saw Smith's red Vette parked in front of it."

"Sure it was Smith's?"

"Had the Manta tag."

"All right. So tell me about this narrow escape from the guy with the gun. And how you knew about him in the first place."

I didn't know exactly where I was going with this, so I decided to try for a smoke screen. "Well, as you know, most warehouses are usually made of aluminum."

206

"And just what does that have to do with any of this?"

"Aluminum is an excellent reflector."

Neil continued looking skeptical.

"Tell him you saw the reflection of the gun from a parked car," Mike said.

I turned slightly again where I thought she was.

"It *might* work," she said.

"Okay. I'll try."

"Try what?" Neil asked suspiciously. "And who're you talking to? Some imaginary entity that might help you with your so-called explanation?"

"In a manner of speaking."

"Tell your invisible friend you're gonna be in some seriously deep shit if this doesn't fly with me."

"You heard him," I told Mike.

"Tell him what I told you," she said.

"Deacon, stop playing games."

"Would you believe I saw the reflection of a gun in a parked car?"

"You've got to be kidding."

"You told me to drop the smartass. I told you I'd tell you the truth. I also said you probably wouldn't believe me."

"Where *was* this parked car?"

"Sitting between the buildings. It was probably a security vehicle, but I can't be sure. It was off-white--"

"All right, there was a vehicle parked between the buildings. So what?"

"How else would I have known about a gun?"

"How the hell am *I* supposed to be convinced there *was* a gun in the first place?"

"Would I make up such a ridiculous story?"

Neil had another swig of coffee, grimaced, then put the cup down and glared at it. "I'm *still* trying to figure out how you spotted that car bomb hooked up to the bottom of your old wreck outside Florida Mall a few weeks back, before you and Papa Joe decided to adopt one another."

"Strange things happen. And my car's a classic."

"And don't forget that story you told me about that knock on your head outside Kelsey's turning you into a Super Private Eye."

"You told me you believed that story."

"Somewhat. Just don't assume I'll believe *everything* you tell me."

A uniform brought in my Beretta .380 and dropped it on Neil's desk.

"Match?" Neil asked.

"Hasn't even been fired recently." Then he left.

"What was *that* all about?" I asked.

"The body in your trunk was killed with a nine-millimeter."

"Really?"

"Two slugs in the pump. Close range."

"My gun's a three-eighty."

"We know that. But I'm sure you realize the three-eighty is just a short version of the nine-millimeter. Which is why your gun was checked."

"Gotcha."

"You didn't by any chance *examine* the body, did you?"

208

"Why would I do that?"

"I don't know. Why would you?"

"Didn't even touch it."

"Forensics aren't gonna find your prints on it, are they?"

"I opened the trunk, saw the body, got scared and really grossed out, then slammed the trunk shut and called you."

Neil stared at me. I could tell he was pulling out a few tidbits that didn't quite make sense. "Did you happen to discover this body somewhere off the Trail, maybe? At a shopping mall?" He'd obviously heard about the anonymous call. "When I was reporting your call, I was told that someone had called in about a suspicious character on Holden Avenue and the Trail, trying to dump a body."

"Would I dump a body, then call you to say I was bringing it in?"

"Maybe you changed your mind."

"And decided it would be much easier to bring it in and go through this uncomfortable grilling for the next three hours, rather than just dump it and drive home?"

Neil thought that over. "Deacon, one day all this fancy backpedaling is gonna get you into trouble."

"I'm being honest with you. I've always been honest with you."

"Always?"

"Except for those few times I had to keep one or two minor things from you. Things I wasn't sure about, of course. But nothing important."

"Like now?"

"I just risked my career to bring in a body."

"You keep the trunk locked, right?"

"Yep."

"Then how'd you know there was a body in your trunk?"

"Tell him the truth," Mike said. I gave her another confused look. "Try it," she said. "It might be the only explanation that actually works."

Mike was right. I pointed to my swollen jaw.

"You were suckered. I got that already."

"And when I woke up, I found myself parked near the dumpster at the shopping mall off of Holden."

"Go on."

My brain went blank. Mike said, "Tell him you had a feeling something was off, so you decided to check your trunk."

"I . . . had this feeling--"

"Here we go again." Neil sat back and shook his head. "Deacon, this mind stuff only goes so far, ya know."

"I just couldn't figure out what happened, so I decided to see if something had been placed in my trunk."

Neil said nothing.

I shrugged. "My head was cloudy."

"It's always cloudy."

"It was worse this time, and I had a headache."

"That whack would've done that."

"Anyway, I couldn't think clearly, but I did wonder what happened, and why I was still alive."

"So you opened the trunk and found the body?"

"More or less."

210

"Sounds reasonable, I guess."

"By the way, how long should it take them to ID the stiff I brought in?"

Neil picked up his phone and spoke softly into it. He said, "That was quick. Thanks." He hung up, then started punching keys. "They already got a match."

"Amazing. And some say the police move like cockroaches stuck in a glue trap."

"I never heard that one."

"I just made it up."

He stopped typing. "Dead man's name was Laurence Simpson Pickett. Thirty-seven years old, in and out of jail the last twenty years for an assortment of unrelated stuff--assault & battery, breaking & entering, selling pot and cocaine. A bungled bank robbery two years ago. Petty shit."

"Bank robbery? Petty?"

"Apparently the bonehead scribbled a note to a teller that said he had a gun in his pocket and wanted ten grand in small bills, but he picked a bank with a silent alarm that went off immediately. He was still waiting for the cashier to give him the money when they stormed in. The idiot had only a Bic lighter and a pack of Trojans in his pockets."

"What was he doing in my trunk?"

"Can't do much else with two slugs in your pump."

"That's not what I meant."

"You have been making a nuisance of yourself the last two days, yes?"

"Me? A nuisance?"

"If you want to hear my theory, put a sock in it and try and act dignified."

"Sometimes you're entirely *too* demanding. But do go on."

"A stiff was dumped in your trunk. All it would've taken was an anonymous call to get us to stop you and open the trunk, and I do believe we received that call. Luckily, you found the stiff first and brought it in yourself. What's all this tell you?"

"I pissed off someone who doesn't want to sweat a murder investigation."

"There ya go."

"But who?"

"Take your pick."

"Please don't tell him Smith's dead," Mike said.

"I know," I told her.

"Know what?" Neil asked sharply.

"Just this. I think Smith's been working on his own. I also think Paseo has no idea what Smith is into and wasn't responsible for the stiff in my trunk."

"Possible. Hard to prove, of course."

"Regardless of who did it, they're gonna be really pissed, now that they know I brought in Pickett on my own."

"How would they know?" Neil asked. "Unless whoever did this has got a connection or two in this building, they have no idea what happened after they dumped the body."

"That's right. If they weren't watching me closely, they *don't* know."

"Even if they *were* watching, they would've had to follow you here to see what went down. They might've followed you, but I don't think they'd want to actually get that close. Criminals aren't usually police station groupies."

"So as far as they know, I'm good for this murder."

"Exactly."

Chapter 18

By the time I left the Station shortly after ten, I was exhausted, my head ached, and my jaw throbbed heavily.

Neil gave me a couple of Aspirin before I left. They hadn't started working yet, but if they weren't doing their job by the time I got back to the apartment, I'd take one of the six Vicodin the dentist gave me last year when I had my root canal. I'd only used one so far. I promised myself I'd only take them for emergencies. And since the pills weren't quite a year old, they'd still have most of their kick left.

As I pulled onto Colonial and drove east, I thought about what Neil and I had discussed earlier and knew it made sense. It also made me more uneasy. You pay to get rid of someone you no longer need by dumping him on someone else who's been pissing you off. Smart. And effective. And if it's done right, you don't even get your hands dirty.

It made me curious about who I'd pissed off. And what this person was involved in. And, of course, Laurence Pickett. Who was he working for? Did he tie in with Florida Exotic Travel? With Alan Smith? With Paseo? And if so, how? And what did the Frazier girl have to do with any of this?

"Hi again." Mike appeared beside me, fully visible.

"I can see you this time."

"Wondering where I've been?"

214

"Actually, I'm wondering who stuck Pickett in my trunk."

"Me, too. When I first saw them dumping the body, I thought it was Smith at first. It was dark, and they'd pulled up directly behind your car, then two of them did it pretty quickly. But when I caught a glimpse of dark hair, I knew it had to be someone else."

"Are you sure Smith is dead?"

"I drifted right in after they'd let him fall to the floor. I took a good, long look. I can tell when someone's dead."

"Did you see his spirit?"

"It had already left."

"He didn't stick around and talk to you?"

"Why would he?"

"I'd think you guys would stick together."

"Why?"

"You're both dead, right?"

"Wouldn't that mean you'd have to stick together with everyone alive?"

"Good point. So where does this leave us?"

"Both Smith and Pickett are dead. That's about all we do know."

***

After Mike had vanished again, I continued the trip home, tired, sore, and a little nervous.

I pulled onto Maguire and drove the next few miles to Lake Underhill, with one eye on the road ahead and the other fixed on the rearview mirror. As I circled the lake, I kept a watchful eye on the traffic behind me. I breathed easier when most of them turned off, but as I sat at the light at the intersection

215

of Conway and Curry Ford, I couldn't help wondering how a small-time hood like Laurence Pickett was involved with Alan Smith. I also wondered if Smith was involved with Jackie Frazier, and if so, how? Could all three of them be tied in with a man I knew only as Paseo? Was I wrong about everything? Was Jackie involved in this *at all*? Or was she just an innocent bystander who only *seemed* to be one of the players?

I realized I should keep my personal feelings out of this. The fact that I didn't like her didn't necessarily mean she was guilty. The fact that she'd dissed me, my car, my age, personality, and everything else, didn't mean she'd taken up with Smith. For all I knew, she might've just slipped down to the bar for a drink and met Smith in passing.

The more I thought about it, the messier and more complicated everything appeared. But even if the girl wasn't involved, some nasty, dangerous people had gone to great lengths to frame me for a murder.

I turned into the shopping center that backs up to the complex property line and parked in front of Jerry's Hardware. Only a couple of lights flickered inside the store. After all, it was ten-thirty. The shopping center was closed as well. Only the drugstore at the opposite end continued doing business.

I flicked off the ignition and doused my lights. I opened the console, took the Beretta out of its holster, and carefully checked the mag and the chamber. Important rule for top-notch detectives and anyone else owning a firearm: Always check your gun after someone else has been messing around with it. The rule goes double if cops were the ones handling it. Cops aren't careful with firearms that don't belong to them. You'd think they would be, but they aren't.

Satisfied the hammer still worked, no one had slobbered on the sight, and all the bullets remained in the clip and pointed in the right direction, I shoved the gun into my pants pocket and got out.

The streetlamp at the corner lit up the hardware store and some of the lot facing the supermarket next to it. About twenty yards of the lot between the east side of the hardware store and Conway Road remained lit. The area extending to my apartment complex sat in darkness.

I went down the concrete thoroughfare and rounded the corner behind the hardware store. Darkness quickly engulfed me. I hadn't brought along my flashlight. You can't sneak around in the shadows very well if you want to use a flashlight.

Carefully dodging discarded shopping carts scattered throughout the lot, I kept a sharp eye on the dimness in front of me, until I reached the end of the lot. A five-foot privacy fence separates the property from the complex. The haze of the streetlamps lighting the apartment buildings comes to within a few feet of the fence.

Cautiously I approached the swing gate. Nothing suspicious, so far. The lights from my kitchen and living room, always left on, showed no movement inside other than the slight flutter of the dining room drapes made by the a/c vent. Outside, a couple of health-minded oldsters braved mosquitoes during their slow laps around the complex. Splashing and squealing emanated from the well-lit pool in the center of the complex. Two middle-aged exercise fanatics used the haze of a streetlight directed at the tennis court in their quest to burn calories. No strange vehicles. No shadows lurking behind the bushes or palmettos.

My cell buzzed just as I got back to the TransAm. It was Phil. "Can you talk now? I've been waiting since seven o'clock for your callback."

I knew better than tell her too much. She was still worried about my head injury and my hallucinations and felt guilty about my near-disaster with Paseo, two kidnappings, plus the fact that I'd been knocked unconscious and left for dead. Phil was always neurotic about such things.

"I just left OPD about twenty minutes ago. They kept me there nearly three hours and I'm really tired."

"I can imagine."

I took one more look behind me and listened carefully, filtering out the Conway traffic and concentrating on approaching footsteps, or the clicking of a gun hammer. Before I got in my car, I scanned the parking lot in front of the supermarket but saw no one. "I'll be fine after I get some sleep."

"Where are you?"

I started up the TransAm and backed out. Still no one lurking about. The night traffic revealed nothing suspicious. "I'm about half a block from my apartment."

"Now you can tell me what happened. You mentioned a body, didn't you? I know the last two days have been kind of crazy and I've been imagining all sorts of weird things, but you *did* mention a body. I'm almost certain you mentioned a body. You *did* mention a body, didn't you?"

Phil had obviously had one or two drinks. She didn't usually ramble. And since she wasn't much of a drinker, it didn't take much to get her fired up.

"What have you been doing?" I asked.

"Pacing the apartment--what else? I can't help wondering what's going on. I'm also worrying myself sick--"

"Besides that."

A pause. "What do you mean, Ralph?"

"Have you . . . had a few?"

"A *few*?"

"Drinks?"

Another pause. "What would make you ask me something like that?"

"Wine?" She hated the taste of whiskey.

I heard her sigh. She was probably silently cursing me for reading her so well. "I . . . had a glass of Chardonnay after dinner."

"Just one?"

"Ralph . . . what does my . . . what does *that* have to do with--"

"You sound a little on edge. I just wondered if you needed an extra glass to help you through."

"Of course I'm on edge. Who *wouldn't* be on edge after all this? Don't you realize how difficult all this has been for me?"

219

Phil usually didn't pull the drama queen routine very often, but when she did, she did it well.

"It hasn't been a picnic for me, either."

She sighed. "I'm sorry, Ralph. I didn't mean--"

"I know, I know. Like I've been trying to tell you, this isn't your fault. Neither of us knew what was happening."

"What *is* happening?"

I parked in my spot and doused the engine and lights. The oldsters passed, their laps much slower. The sounds of splashing and squealing in the complex pool had died down a little. The exercise fanatics had already fled the tennis court.

"Ralph?"

"From what I've learned, I just happened to stumble upon a shady bunch by being in the wrong places at the wrong times."

"Then you think there might be a good chance Jackie isn't involved in any of this?"

"There's a chance. I don't know how good it is. Not yet, anyway."

"Well, if it means anything, the party was a complete success. Jack and Ruth both thanked me and my team for all we did."

"Did he mention his daughter?"

"Only that she had a great time and that she can't wait to take her first trip to Disney this weekend."

"They're taking her to *Disney?*"

"Jack doesn't have the time. He has to fly to Miami tomorrow morning on business. He didn't say how long he'll be there, but it sounded important."

220

"Hmmm. . ."

"Are you saying that could actually *mean* something?"

"Everything means something, Phil. In this business, every little thing is important."

"Then what's it mean?"

"I don't know yet."

"Then how do you know it's important?"

"I have to think more about it. Then I have to figure it out. Once I put it all together, I have to decide if it fits."

"I think I understand. So . . . what are you going to do now?"

"First of all, I'm going to check out my apartment to see if anyone's been there."

"You do that a lot, as I remember."

"Part of the job."

"Yes. It's horrible. And aggravating. I clearly remember the many times you used to get up in the middle of the night to check on things."

"And when I came back to bed, what did we do then?"

Silence. I liked it when I could rattle her cage, even if it was only for a second.

"What's next on your itinerary?" she asked finally.

"If someone's been there, I'll take it from there. If not, I plan to have a few stiff belts, maybe two or three more pieces of my mother's *biscotti,* then off to bed."

"How is she, by the way?"

"Just fine."

"Still calling you every other day?"

221

"You could say that."

"I've always liked her, Ralph."

"She likes you, too." I hated when Phil got sloppy. "Anyway, those are my plans for tonight."

"That sounds sensible. And you do need sleep. I can tell you're exhausted."

"I'm pretty tired, all right. Want to come over and help--"

"Ralph. . ."

"Sure you don't want to make sure I can find my way to the bed? I *am* awfully tired."

"I'm sure."

"Positive?"

"Ralph . . . we're divorced, remember?"

"How can I forget? You keep reminding me."

"We're not supposed to be doing things like that anymore."

"I figured it was worth a shot."

"Good night, Ralph."

"How about if I come over there?"

"Keep in touch, now."

I hung up. Ex-wives could be really stubborn at times. I got out of my car and walked up the path to my front stoop, bent, and tilted the wicker basket I keep near the front door for newspapers and magazine deliveries. I have a spare key concealed in a small brown flap of scrap canvas I designed myself and stapled to the bottom of the basket. Since my keys were taken from me earlier, I had to use it. I made a mental note to have my lock changed as soon as possible.

The apartment was cool, comfortable, and-- most of all--empty. After a quick but thorough walk-through, I slipped the chain in its slot and dead-bolted the door. For the next couple of minutes, I listened with my ear to the door, occasionally squinting at the peephole just to make sure. I knew I was being paranoid, but I didn't want to take chances. After all, someone out there had my keys.

I crossed the dining room and grabbed the bottle of Jack's I keep on the kitchen counter. Despite the aspirins Neil gave me in his office, my head still pounded, so I elected to save myself the aggravation of looking for a clean glass and drank right from the bottle. The fiery liquor raced down my limbs, warming my gut and sending sizzling blasts into my lower limbs. I had another healthy swallow. This one reached my tingling jaw and relaxed me even more. Maybe I wouldn't need a Vicodin after all.

I opened Mom's Tupperware container and hungrily eyed her *biscotti*. It was only then that I realized I hadn't eaten since that one tangy mouthful of the burrito before Mr. Human Sledgehammer put my lights out. I reluctantly closed the container. I love *biscotti*, but unless you dunk the hell out of them, they require serious jaw action. I placed a couple of slices of lunchmeat and some soft cheese on a piece of soft bread. If I kept this up, I'd have to start shopping for smaller clothes. Being small is not good when you need to intimidate people to do your job effectively. In this age of tall, broad-shouldered heroes and huge, steroid-laden athletes, people don't respect or fear a normal-sized guy running around, asking irritating questions. And when I did finally make the trip to Lauderdale to visit Mom and the relatives, she'd immediately launch into a relentless quest to fatten me up as quickly as possible.

I had another slug of Jack's, stepped into the shower, and stood under the warm spray for nearly twenty minutes. Mindful of the stinging tap to the back of my skull, I blotted my hair lightly with the towel. Even though I knew full well that my jaw would probably scare the shit out of me, I stepped up to the mirror anyway. My cheek still gave the impression I was storing walnuts. It also had turned a nasty blue-green shade. I decided to take a Vicodin to be safe.

Since I needed to empty my mind of all unnecessary baggage and direct my efforts toward a good night's sleep, I decided on Brubeck for tonight's serenade. I'd been a jazz buff for years and have quite a collection of jazz and big band CDs. I use different artists for my many different moods. I put on Louis Armstrong for particularly bad days, Miles and Coltrane for frustrating days. I use Maynard Ferguson when I'm feeling good and Doc Severinsen when I'm feeling terrific. Clifford Brown, Cat Anderson, and Chet Baker are all perfect for a romantic evening. You can't do better than Don Ellis when you want to get drunk or high, turn off the lights, and see things that aren't there. I also play the harmonica whenever I want to unwind and just mellow.

Tonight would not be a good night for my harmonica. For one thing, I was too exhausted. And my swollen jaw would protest too much. Brubeck never failed to relax me after a long, hard day. I even slept better after falling asleep listening to good ol' Dave.

I took my "Greatest Hits" CD from the stack on the player in the living room. Then, after one last glance at the peephole and a quick check of the chain on the door, I slipped the disc into my compact player on the bedroom dresser.

I got into bed, turned off the lights, focused my thoughts away from cold, frustrating reality, and let the soft, gentle strains of "Take Five" lull me into a deep, dark sleep.

Chapter 19

The ringing of my cell phone awoke me. It was Neil Haversack.

"What time is it?"

"Why, it's past nine. Don't tell me I *woke* you, Sleeping Beauty. . ."

I rubbed my eyes. Parallel needles of sparkling sunlight penetrating the horizontal blinds told me Neil could be right. The clock on the nightstand gave me the same news: 9:18. Despite my uneasiness, I'd slept through the night. Dave Brubeck had once again proven himself The Man.

"I had to get up to answer the phone anyway," I told Neil, and yawned.

"I've got something you might be interested in."

"What's it about?"

"Your boy Pickett, to start with."

I wasn't sure I liked Neil's tone. I sensed all sorts of weird things happening again. "Let me guess. He's not really dead."

"Deacon, you hungover or something? You're not making any sense."

"When have I ever not made sense?"

"Let's not get into that. Just shake the sleep out of your noggin. I'll wait."

I sat up. An avalanche of warm pain pulsated on the left side of my face. I gently touched my jaw. It hurt, but not nearly as badly as the night before. I probably needed another Vicodin.

"Deacon? You there?"

"More or less." Fighting the pain, I struggled into a standing position and tried not to sway. I knew better than close my eyes. I'd done that once before and ended up face-down on the floor. I was smarter now. Older. Wiser. Once I got the gravity issue licked, I padded down the carpeted hall, heading to the kitchen.

"Deacon? What're you doing?"

"Taking something for my jaw."

"Still hurt?"

"You saw it last night. What do *you* think?"

"You ought to stop using your face for a punching bag."

"I generally use the back of the head for that. Yesterday I thought I'd try something different."

"You really need to start learning how to protect yourself."

"It's hard doing that when someone's sneaking up on you."

"You need eyes in the back of your head. Go buy a dog."

"What do I do when I have to go inside a building? I leave the dog outside, someone steals him, then I come back out and someone sneaks up on me again."

"I admire your optimism. Try learning to be more careful anyway. You never know. It might save your life."

I dry-swallowed a Vicodin and leaned against the kitchen counter, waiting for it to dissolve and start working. "I'll give it a try, but as they say, everyone needs a hobby."

"Like I've told you before, try stamp-collecting."

"Boring."

"Getting beat up appeals more to you?"

"It's a form of masochism I never outgrew as a child. It comes from being brought up Catholic."

"Be serious for a change. I managed to find out a few things about Pickett."

I went into the living room and lay down on the sofa. "I'm listening."

"Pickett was arrested three months ago for assault and battery on a prostitute outside an Orlando bar. He needed ten grand to post his bond. Apparently he had some other charges pending--three DUIs, some speeding tickets, and two drunk and disorderlies. The presiding judge had dealt with him before and decided to go harsher."

"What's the punch line to this?"

"His bail was paid by a woman we can tie in to Jason Dean."

"Never heard of him."

"I did a little digging. Dean's an egghead. A computer whiz. He graduated from UCF twelve years ago with a Master's in Computer Analysis and Diagnostics."

"What's the connection here?"

"Dean's no shrinking violet himself. He's been convicted of computer hacking and software piracy, even spent a few months in the slammer for the last hacking charge."

"I didn't know they were cracking down on stuff like that."

"The Feds tend to get their blood up when you hack into their mainframe and start screwing around with sensitive material."

"So Dean's an arrogant geek. Don't call Ripley just yet. All geeks are conceited assholes."

"Dean's also an addict. Mostly cocaine and pills, but he's also done heroin and LSD. He got into serious trouble with the cocaine a few months back when he tried selling to an undercover agent. He's been clean since. He's been seen in bars a few times. We're assuming he saw the light and picked booze because it's safer. And legal."

"Where's the connection with Pickett?"

"I'm figuring that since Pickett was also a boozer, the two probably met in a bar."

"I guess that's possible, but what else have you got?"

"Dean's ex-wife was mugged at a Publix supermarket shortly after Dean was released by the Feds. She didn't see who did it, but a couple of shoppers did, and they did a composite here at OPD. Guess who the likeness favors?"

"You think Dean pissed off Pickett?"

"Actually, I'm thinking Dean offered Pickett a job."

"Isn't that a bit of a stretch?"

"It would be, if his ex hadn't withdrawn her petition for alimony that same week."

"Ah. Not much of a stretch at all."

"Something else I found out. About a year or so ago, Dean started up a software company and runs an office in downtown Orlando."

I ignored the sudden dizziness and sat up. "It wouldn't be A&D Software, would it?"

"You're really good when you're not clowning around," Neil said flatly.

"My brain is clearer when I'm in pain."

"So you slam it into a wall whenever you want to figure something out?"

"Only when the computer's down and I can't get into Google."

"Deacon, you worry me. But let's get back to Pickett. . ."

"We could both be totally off-base here, you know. Pickett could be one of those poor unfortunates that society is always talking about. You know. A product of his upbringing--"

"My educated guess would vote on A&D Software being just a front, like your Florida Exotic Travel. They might do just enough sub work to stay legit with the IRS and make their rent."

"I'm pretty sure neither are legit businesses. I just don't know where to go from there."

"I keep telling you to walk away from this mess, but since you never listen, I'd say Dean would be a good guess. Follow up on him and see where that takes you."

"No one can link Dean to Pickett?"

"Nothing solid."

"You think Dean posted Pickett's bail for the mugging?"

"A young woman sprang Pickett. We figured she was probably a girlfriend of Dean's. She did everything she could to stay anonymous--paid cash, used a fake ID, and provided no address. Just a P.O.

Box. From what they said at the bail office, she was a knockout. The tall, leggy type."

"I guess Dean didn't want anyone linking him with Pickett."

"Common sense tells us he was probably using Pickett for jobs Dean didn't want to bother with. Pickett had shady connections. When you know someone with shady connections and you're not exactly the Honest Abe type yourself, this can lead to a beautiful friendship."

"Especially when you keep your association secret."

"Did I mention that Pickett had traces of high-quality coke in his pockets?"

"High-quality?"

"Our lab guys said they hadn't seen this sort of stuff in a while. Said it was about as pure as you can find. Last they'd seen similar stuff, they remembered it coming from the West Coast."

The West Coast. The hair on the back of my neck tingled. "Strange, someone like Pickett handling anything high-quality."

"My sentiments exactly."

"So tell me more about the girl who posted Pickett's bond."

"She was definitely an ex-girlfriend of Dean's. She came into the Station a couple of weeks ago with her jaw wired shut and a black eye. Said she was mugged by a guy fitting Pickett's description."

"Didn't she realize that would make her look suspicious? I mean, she springs the guy, then comes back in a few weeks later to say he rearranged her face."

"They said she was really upset when she came in. Seriously pissed, as one of my friends said. You don't do that kind of damage to a woman's face--especially when she's a knockout. She'll go right for your balls."

Something was slightly off. "Didn't she care about that getting back to Dean?"

"We can't be sure, but either someone got to her, or she skipped town. She hasn't been seen or heard from since."

The coke issue nagged at me. "How about this? She's the one who brought in the high-quality blow. If she's trafficking for Dean, she might be back on the West Coast. Or in Miami. Or anywhere else they decide to supply."

"If Dean was the one who had her marked up, she wouldn't want to work for him, she'd want him dead. Otherwise, she'd make serious tracks."

"That might have been the result of a burn. You never know. Maybe Pickett got greedy and marked her up to scare Dean."

"But if Dean doesn't scare, he calls Pickett's bluff. He might even be really pissed that his girl's no longer perfect, so he pays someone to do Pickett, dumps the body, and this balances the books."

"Any luck with the slugs you found?"

"Not yet."

"I'm wondering why they didn't use my gun. They wanted to frame me. That would've made everything easy."

"That's the problem with frame-ups. The better the frame, the more amateur it looks. The best kind of frame has loose ends dangling all over the place. That keeps us busy for weeks."

"Maybe they didn't have time. If it was just a dump job, they'd be in a hurry."

"They had time to knock you out, shoot Pickett, toss him in your trunk, then drive you several miles in heavy Orlando traffic and drop you off. How much more time would it have taken to toss Pickett in your trunk, use your gun, then drop you off?"

"Maybe they were nervous."

"Why?"

"They're computer geeks just starting out in a brand-new career. They haven't gotten the hit thing down yet. Or maybe doing in Smith and Pickett spooked them."

"Maybe they just didn't want to bother with your gun."

"No prints on it other than mine?"

"Nope."

"They *were* in a hurry, then."

"What you just said could mean a lot."

"What did I say?"

"About them not bring pros. Just starting out. Being nervous."

"I'm pretty bright sometimes, huh?"

"Sometimes. Other times you can be really stupid."

"My biorhythm swings both ways."

"And other times you just use your head for batting practice."

"You've got a point. But I think I'm right-on with this. Pros would've used my gun, or at least taken it and used it on someone else."

"So this tells us we're dealing with perps who might be smart in some ways, but morons in others."

"I wonder if they know they're muscling in on Raguzzo's territory."

Neil sighed. "We're not sure Raguzzo's involved in the escort business."

"Mobs almost always have the local pros nailed down tight."

"That doesn't actually prove Raguzzo's involved--"

"He's involved in just about everything else. He could have a few of his men dabbling in it. Maybe on their own. Maybe our computer geeks could be doing something you're always accusing me of doing."

"You mean getting in over your head?"

Sometimes Neil could be bright, too. "Exactly."

"So what's the next step?"

"Our two arrogant geeks need to be indoctrinated."

Neil went silent. I could hear him fidgeting in his seat. Neil always fidgeted whenever he heard something that sounded illegal or shady. "I'm neither condoning nor listening to any of this. I'm not even one hundred percent sure what you just said."

"I *said*--"

"Don't want to *hear* it."

"By the way, did you find out anything else about A&D? I wouldn't mind hearing what the A stands for."

"The CEO's name is Armstrong. Peter Armstrong. Tell you anything?"

Mike had mentioned a man referred to only as Pete. This had suddenly become much clearer.

***

After Neil hung up, I stepped into the shower.

The Vicodin was already working, so I experienced no surprises or additional pain as the warm spray assaulted my face. I immediately began feeling better. Razor in hand, I stepped up to the mirror. Should I or shouldn't I? Forcing a razor blade over my tender jaw and slapping the nicks and cuts with cologne would definitely aggravate my injury. I decided to try the grubby look for the day's fashion statement. Besides, a beard makes me appear rugged.

I had a light breakfast of soft eggs and coffee, keeping the chewing to a minimum and passing on the toast for obvious reasons. I also decided to pass on my morning floss and tooth-brushing. Nothing wrong with a good mouthwash rinse and calling it good. I didn't exactly have a heavy date later on. And since Phil had turned me down again last night, I didn't plan on getting lucky for a while.

My first errand of the day, of course, was a quick jaunt to the apartment office to ask the manager to make arrangements for a locksmith to change the locks on my door. He didn't squawk much--he knew how I earned my living. Besides, I'd done this same thing twice before. I was paying for it, so there was no problem. His only inconvenience was the phone call and the fifty-yard hike to my apartment to greet the locksmith when

235

he showed up. Besides, it got him out of the office for a little while.

I got in the TransAm. It was time to use my sparkling personality to get a few tricky things done that I couldn't possibly accomplish on my own. Or with the help of OPD.

***

Vesper's Vixens, built on several acres of prime Orlando real estate, sits a hundred yards off the main highway, facing a sprawling gravel parking lot.

Porsches, Mercedes, Jaguars, Lexus's, and Corvettes fill many spaces in the front lot. The huge stucco building's deep-blue Spanish tile roof can be seen a mile away. Its front doors are made of polished oak, its canvas portico a rich red. White marble pillars give the structure a royal appearance. Potted plants placed at three-foot intervals line the front stoop.

Papa Joe Raguzzo owned Vesper's, as well as several other clubs, massage parlors, and restaurants in the Central Florida area. He also owned clubs in Tampa and Miami, and two gambling casinos in Biloxi, Mississippi. I'd stumbled across Papa Joe a few weeks ago, not long after Mike had popped into my life. Thanks to a quirk of fate, I managed to land on his good side. I hadn't known at the time that a Mob boss even *had* a good side, but my being half-Italian certainly helped.

Surviving a car bomb a couple of his men had rigged under my TransAm helped as well. Spotting something only a trained bomb expert could find impresses a Mob boss. But if Raguzzo or anyone

236

else found that it was Mike who'd actually discovered the bomb, I'd be in serious trouble. Like most Italians, Papa Joe was superstitious. He'd probably freak if he suspected an actual guardian angel was looking out for me.

I didn't know if Papa Joe knew about Dean or Armstrong. If he didn't, he should be told. I was a private detective, not an informer. I was supposed to be on the right side of the law. However, I considered it necessary to rid the city of two inept thugs who'd already been responsible for at least two murders. I was reasonably certain they were also responsible for my being kidnapped twice in two days, knocked unconscious twice, and nearly framed for murder.

The Mob is not your typical benevolent society. I knew what they did to rid themselves of competition and irritations. After learning a few things from Neil, on my own, and with Mike's help, I didn't think I had much of a choice. Getting Raguzzo involved was the only way I knew to bring this nasty business to an abrupt end.

Mike joined me just as I was about to get out of the TransAm, appearing in denim shorts, a pink tank top, and open-toed white pumps. She looked fabulous. "Slumming again?" I asked. "By the way, your legs are delicious."

"Thank you. But don't get worked up. I'm dead, remember?"

"That's not much of an issue when you've got legs like that."

"I don't like you coming here, you know. Bad vibes."

"I won't be long."

"What are you planning to do?"

"Stir the pot."

"Every time you do that, you end up unconscious."

"Well, it's like this. I've come just about as far as I can on my own. I need help."

"Help? From mob guys?"

"I can't ask the cops because I don't know what's going on, and cops won't come into the picture unless you've got solid evidence. All I know is that some idiots are doing a bunch of bad things, and each time I try to find out what they're doing, they do nasty things to me. I've decided to turn the tables."

"So what do you think these mob guys will do?"

"Ever take a shovelful of fire ants from one mound and dump it on another?"

"I can't hold a shovel, silly."

"It makes for some really impressive fireworks."

Since it wasn't quite noon, only the first three rows of the parking lot were filled. I parked two rows down, between a silver Porsche and a classic Camaro GT, and walked down the gravel path. Two no-necked steroid freaks in ill-fitting suits guarded the entrance like giant Rottweilers. They stood beneath the canopy, blocking the double doorway. I didn't recognize either of them from my last visit, but that was nothing new. The turnover rate for steroid freaks working in strip clubs is just as heavy as with Walmart greeters. I walked up to the one in front and waited for the usual exchange.

"Ten bucks, cover," he said, his huge palm moving in my direction like a crane bucket about to scoop up a heavy load.

"Better not be facing anyone when one of those shirt buttons pops," I told his ribcage. "You'll put someone's eye out."

He just grunted in reply. Steroid freaks aren't generally known for their gift of gab.

I dropped the bill into his palm. It disappeared as the hand instantly turned into a concrete block-sized fist, sliding downward and disappearing in his pants pocket.

"Go on in." Looking equally bored, his massive boyfriend eased open the heavy oak door.

"They both have nice butts," Mike said.

"Behave."

The place was cool, dark, and moderately quiet. The juke played something from an old Michael Jackson video. Two skinny naked girls danced on the bar beneath the flickering strobe lights. Half a dozen well-dressed male customers in the large room followed the scantily clad waitresses around while the others sat at the bar, drooling at the dancing bar girls.

"They've got nothing on you," I told Mike.

"Flattery won't work. I still don't think you should be here."

Sonny Bergman had been managing Vesper's for the last three years. Since it was commonly known that he wasn't exactly a people person, talking to him was going to be tricky. Convincing him to let me talk to Raguzzo would be even trickier.

Mike and I walked up to the bar. The barman was also someone I'd never seen before. He was older than most of the other male employees, about forty, and had the look of an ex-serviceman. A couple of tatts covered his corded forearms. Probably ex-Navy or former Marine.

"I'll have a Jack's on ice."

"Somebody belt ya?" He frowned at my jaw.

"I dropped my keys."

"Huh?"

"When I bent to pick them up, someone decided to open the door. The knob caught me square in the jaw."

"Son of a bitch." He grabbed a bottle from the stack, found a clean glass, added ice, and fixed my drink. When he came back, I slipped him a ten-spot. "Sonny in?" I asked, and he shrugged.

"Does that mean he's not in? Does it mean he is and you don't want to tell me? Or does it mean you honestly don't know?"

Another shrug.

"Does that mean I'm right? Or is it your way of telling me to mind my own--"

"How's your drink?"

I had a sip. "Strong."

"I'm happy you like it." His bored expression did not change.

"That's your happy?"

He shrugged.

"I'm so glad you explained yourself. I was actually worried your biorhythm could be messed up a tad."

"You trying to rile me, Mister?"

"Please be careful," Mike whispered in my ear.

"Is it working?"

"Lemme know when you want another drink."

"Does that mean you're not going to tell me if Sonny's in?"

"I don't *know* if he's in, Slick."

"The name's Deacon. Can you possibly find out? Maybe with a cell phone or some other form of high-tech communication?"

"Deacon?" His dark eyebrows squished closer together.

"You're paying attention. I like that. It suggests character and poise. Also, a fair amount of useable brain cells. But I really would like to find out if Sonny's in. It would be the highlight of my day. I have to tell him something important."

He turned his back. I didn't see his arm move, but he held a cell phone against his ear.

"Now I understand why you get in so much trouble," Mike said.

"Sometimes you've got to break some legs to make an omelet."

"I'm glad I'm not able to have breakfast with you."

A moment later the barman turned and put both hands on the bar counter. Neither held the cell phone. "Sonny'll give you one minute."

"It's all I need." I finished my drink. Someone tapped me on the shoulder. A steroid freak dwarfed

241

me just three feet away, looking down at me. In the darkness, his lower lip seemed to be salivating. I wondered if he'd been fed lately. "*You're* not Sonny, are you?" I'd heard Sonny was big, but not a muscle freak.

"Somebody belt ya?"

"I pissed off my girlfriend and she decided to end the argument by tossing a bowling ball at my face."

"*Damn*." He extended an arm. "This way."

Mike and I followed him down the dark hall, which led to the bathrooms, pay phones, a few offices, and one marked Manager. I had a flash of *déjà vu* from a few weeks ago, when I found myself in this same setting moments before I ended up unconscious.

"He's scary," Mike said. "You only come up to his chin."

"Thanks for noticing."

"Good things come in small packages."

I knew she meant well, but I said nothing. A guy doesn't like hearing that from a female--not even when she's dead.

Mr. Human Muscle reached out and pushed open the door for me. Such a gentleman. Mike and I went in.

Sonny Bergman must have changed his name from something like Santino Bergetti, or Alphonse Berlinetta. He looked like DeNiro in his fat scenes from *Raging Bull*. Sonny was around six-two and went probably close to three hundred pounds. He looked me up and down, then stopped at my jaw. A blank expression covered his face. "Deacon?"

242

"Yeah."

"*Rafaello* Deacon?"

"I like Ralph better."

"What happened to your fucking jaw?"

These guys weren't very subtle, but they sure were observant. "I tried to catch an alligator and its tail nailed me."

He grimaced. "Dumb."

I shrugged. "I do strange things when I'm drunk."

"So whaddya want?"

"I just came to tell you something your boss should know."

He'd blinked at the word *boss*. "Keep talking."

"I think I might know some people who're trying to get something together in the area."

"And why should my boss care about this?"

"They're starting up an escort service and are probably going after the big wigs flying in. They're using a new limousine service on North Semoran."

"And ya think my boss cares?"

"I'm just telling you in case the subject comes up."

"And what's *your* interest in this?"

"Your boss and I know one another. He respects me, I respect him. He's been watching out for me. The least I can do is watch out for him."

Sonny nodded. Italians tended to get corny when you stroked their egos. They were criminals, but had a code, nonetheless. "Thanks for the word."

"One other thing. Whoever's doing this might also be bringing in some high-quality cocaine. I

243

don't know how much, only that it's good stuff and probably comes from the West Coast."

Mike and I barely reached my car before my cell buzzed.

"Already?" Mike asked.

"They work fast when they feel threatened." I flicked on my cell.

"Deacon?"

I recognized the gravelly Robert Loggia-like voice instantly. I slid in behind the wheel and rolled down the windows to let in a fresh batch of stifling heat. "Speaking."

"I hear you're at one of my clubs, irritating my people."

"That depends on what you mean by irritating."

"This line bugged?"

"You sure are paranoid."

"Hey, you make a shitload of enemies to get where I'm at. The better the enemy, the more paranoid you get."

"I thought we were friends."

"You're a regular *paisano*, Rafaello. But you're still a fucking cop."

"Private."

"A fucking cop, anyway."

"And it's Ralph."

"Why you no like the name Rafaello? Your momma gave it to you."

"This is America. American kids can't handle a name like that."

"Fuck 'em. Rafaello's a good, noble name, my friend."

244

"This is America, and when you toss a name like Rafaello at a bunch of kids named Steve, Bob, Bill, and Fred, it's like waving the red flag at the bull."

"Fuck 'em."

"I wanted to shoot them. But all that happened before school shootings became fashionable."

His chuckle sounded more like a grunt. "So what's this bullshit about someone trying to muscle in on my territory?"

"Ever heard of Florida Exotic Travel? North Semoran Limousine Service?"

"What about 'em?"

"I think they're both fronts for a new escort service. Two computer geeks are running it. They work from a dummy computer business in the Orlando Center Building off Magnolia. A&D Software. Names are Jason Dean and Peter Armstrong. There were three of them, but now there are only two."

"And you think I'm interested in this escort service because I'm a successful businessman? Or because I own limousines?"

"I just thought you might be interested in what's going on. They're computer geeks, but they're also crazy. They could be involved in at least two murders."

"Computer geeks? Murderers? What's this fucking town turning into?"

"A cesspool of psychos and sociopaths."

"You been to the cops? Tell them about all this?"

245

"I thought I'd tell you first, give you a heads-up. Buddies share, right?"

"I appreciate it, *paisano*, I really do. But this bullshit doesn't involve me."

"Sorry about that. Like I said, I thought you ought to know."

"No problem. How's your momma?"

"She sends her regards."

"You . . . *told* her about me?"

"No."

"Then--"

"Just a joke. I'm a funny guy, remember?"

"How could I forget?"

"You're old. You forget things."

"I remember what's important, smartass. Know what I remember most about you?"

"What's that?"

"You're a *stronzone* as well as a smartass."

"I take after my father."

"You're more Dago than Mick."

"You saying I'm more like my mother?"

"Show some respect for the lady that brought you into this world. I'll reach through this phone and slap you silly."

"Too late for that."

"Maybe one day you and I get together again, have some *vino*. Discuss things. You tell me what's bugging you and I'll tell you what's bugging me."

"Sounds good. I still haven't sampled the food at Dante's."

"Our food's the best in the city."

"I've heard."

"When you wanna meet?"

"*You* pick the time."

"I'll let you know."

"Sounds like a plan."

"One thing."

"What's that?"

"Don't bring your piece next time. Guns make me nervous."

"Me, too."

"Then why'd you bring one last time? You wouldn't've been able to take it out, *capisc*? I let you keep it just so you'd feel better. I run a classy place. No need for guns there."

"I had no choice. Someone kept trying to kill me and I wanted to be prepared."

"That someone's retired now. He's back in the old country, watering his plants. No need to be nervous or prepared."

"Really?"

"You have my word. Know what that means?"

"It means I'm not going to die while I'm in your place, talking to you."

"You learn fast, *paisano*."

Chapter 20

Mike and I got back to my apartment at around one-thirty.

A note was stuck to my door. I recognized the stationery--the complex logo in the center at the top, with the Florida sun hiding behind a palm tree at the bottom left corner. The same sort of tackiness you see on most Florida postcards. The note said:

Pick up your new keys at the office.

The Management

I picked them up, left my money with Mona, the office's constantly bored part-time secretary with the huge bouffant hairdo, then went back to my place. I couldn't help noticing Mike's disapproving look as I picked up the bottle of Jack's. "I've had a stressful morning. I deserve a good belt."

"Just don't overdo it."

"You're not trying to sound like my mother, are you?"

"I just don't want you to get drunk. It's early in the day. What if that mob guy calls back and you have to go somewhere? You don't want to leave here drunk, do you?"

I hated to admit it, but she was right. I put down the bottle, then went into the kitchen to make lunch. Since I still wasn't ready to subject my aching jaw to my mother's crunchy *biscotti*, I decided on a ham and Swiss on rye. Maybe I could catch an old movie on the tube. If not, the Garden Guy might be doing one of his shows. I loved the Garden Guy. He really knew his shit about gardening.

Anyway, I'd done enough damage for one afternoon and wanted to relax. Papa Joe was probably already finding out things that would make his blood pressure rise. My aim in life was to irritate the right people at the right time and do whatever it took to shake up those who needed it.

I opened the freezer to get out the bread. My cell buzzed. The display said *Unknown name, unknown number*. I clicked it on. "Deacon here."

"Why the hell didn't you tell me a female's running this bogus operation?" barked Raguzzo in his loud, agitated voice.

"What are you talking about?"

"You know damn well what I'm talking about, *paisano*. A female's calling the shots on this."

"On what?"

"What, you acting *stupido* now?"

It was coming to me, but much slower than I wanted it to. I was still thinking about that sandwich and the Garden Guy. I needed to switch my priorities and focus on reality.

"Is that who I think it is?" Mike asked. "That Mob guy?" I nodded. She shook her head, frowned, and drifted down the hall.

"You're talking about the escort service?" I asked Papa Joe.

"What the hell *else* should I be talking about? You tell me about two computer dorks trying to muscle in on my town and I find out they're being led around by their dicks by some slut."

Despite my suspicions, I chose to sound stupid and clueless. As I've said many times before, stupid and clueless actually works. "I didn't know."

249

Silence. He was probably trying to decide if I was telling him the truth. "We *paisanos,* yeah?"

"That's why I went to Vesper's. I wanted to tell you what I knew. You know how dangerous that was for me, right? All those steroid freaks wandering around, looking to hurt someone they think is causing trouble? I could've been *killed*, dammit. Or at least seriously messed up."

"They know to call me first. They do anything to you without my okay, they're in big trouble."

"They know that, right?"

"Fucking A, they know."

"What if they don't know who I am?"

"You told 'em, yeah?"

"I told them."

"Then there should be no problem. They mess you up for no reason, they answer to me. Unless you're playing me for a *stronzone*, that's how it is now."

"I didn't know all that. I just went in there, looking to talk to Sonny."

"You no feeding me the bullshit, then?"

"I didn't *think* I was."

"I can tell when someone's lying to me."

"I'm not lying."

"Listen, *paisano*, I know how dangerous it is to let some bimbo lead you around by your dick. When she's done with it, she's done with you."

"Some guys never learn."

"Some guys are dickheads."

"But what does it matter if a female's involved? It's still something you needed to know, right?"

"Mebbe. . ."

250

"Then what's the problem?"

"This line bugged?"

"And here we just proclaimed our undying love and admiration for one another. . ."

"You okay, Deacon?"

"That's a matter of opinion. But no, I never use bugs. You ought to know that by now."

"Just checking. Force of habit."

"Yeah, I know. So what's the problem?"

"I no like dealing with no female. They're fucking crazy. They make you all kinds of funny and messed up by making you worry about your dick. They bump against you to get you all upset and pissed off, and before you know it, you're doing stupid things you haven't done since you were a fucking idiot kid. Females are no good for a business relationship. They take away our manhood. How can we be men without our manhood?"

"Your point?"

"We need to make some sort of arrangement here."

"I'll buy that."

"Okay. We're on the same page. All we need to do is find some way of putting this irritation behind us."

"Tell me about this female."

"Some hoity-toity piece says her papa's some Orlando big shot lawyer and knows a bunch of first-class big shots. Bitch has got a mouth on her. Trailer trash stuff. She had those computer dorks wrapped around her little finger and when they came up missing, she turned nasty. Made my boys *blush*, for Chrissakes."

251

This was getting interesting. "Have *you* seen her?"

"Hell, no. I can't be bothered with this. I sent over a couple of my men from one of my clubs--"

"Did they tell you what she looks like?"

"Little bitch, not much meat on her. Blond hair, streaked and glittered, makes her look like a clown. Tramp stamps and silver all over her. A fucking *nose* ring, for Chrissakes. Maybe her papa *is* rich, but she still looks like a slut."

It was the Frazier brat all along. Why wasn't I surprised? I took a deep breath to keep from laughing.

"You okay?" Mike asked, drifting back in the room. I nodded. She said, "You look like you're ready to turn blue."

"Deacon? You still there?"

I took more deep breaths. Laughing right now would not be cool. When Raguzzo was boiling mad, you didn't want him to think you were laughing at him. Italians hated being laughed at--especially rich ones with bad tempers and bad men on their payroll who killed folks and messed them up. "I'm . . . still here."

"You were right about that limo service and the dummy travel agency."

"What about the coke?"

"Haven't found it. Not yet, anyway. But we will--especially if it's as good as you say. I got some people on the West Coast I deal with. Business ventures--ya know?"

"Yeah, I know."

"Anyway, something like this could interfere with our interests, so we got to see about it and investigate, make sure it doesn't get in our way."

"What happened with the agency?"

"They came up with a sudden cash flow problem."

"Bummer."

"It happens when you start up a business without checking out the competition first. When the competition's already set up, *they* got all the contacts. Without contacts, you're fucked. Get it?"

"Got it."

"See, without contacts, you might as well pack your bags. And when your competitors tell you that you really *should* pack your bags, you better listen."

"*I* would."

"That's because you're no computer punk with an attitude. You're a smartass, but you're manageable. When you *ain't* manageable, that's when your competition decides you're a problem. You know what the competition does with problems, right, Rafaello?"

"Ralph. The competition gets rid of problems."

"Or turns them into *tiny* ones."

"So I take it this is no longer a problem."

"No longer a *big* one."

"So . . . what are you saying?"

"*You're* gonna take care of this one for me."

"Let me guess. I'm going to do this real soon, right?"

Raguzzo chuckled. "Like I said before, *paisano*, you learn fast."

***

253

Just as Raguzzo had said, Mike and I found Jackie Frazier at the Hilton in Disney Village, in a room on the third floor.

Maybe she *had* intended to visit Disney, as she'd told her parents. But somehow this just didn't matter right now. She'd gotten herself involved with the wrong people, and if she wasn't steered in the right direction, she was going to die a quick death. And all the money and connections in the world wouldn't help her.

One of Raguzzo's men stood outside the door when Mike and I got out of the elevator. I could tell he was connected to Raguzzo by his dark features and huge shoulders. And also by the look of total boredom on his face.

"She in there?" I asked. A nod. "She been a problem?" Another nod. I grabbed the doorknob. "You ain't seen nothing yet."

She was dressed in a red tank top, designer jeans, and athletic shoes. A green Gators cap was shoved sideways onto her head in the same fashion as a street punk, or stupid kid. She sat slumped in one of those stylish but really uncomfortable wing chairs that costs as much as the average house payment.

Another one of Raguzzo's men stood beside her, watching me, his bored expression like the guy guarding the door. The girl's skinny arms were crossed over her chest. Her slender legs were also crossed. Her makeup was smeared, especially around the eyes. She looked like she'd been crying. It took her a few seconds to recognize me. When she finally did, her eyes narrowed. "*You?*"

254

"That's what everyone calls me." I smiled pleasantly and tried very hard not to look triumphant. "How are things in O-Town?"

"*You're* the one responsible for these . . . *goons* . . . keeping me here against my will?"

"I really can't take credit for that. But thanks for the thought."

"I *knew* you were an asshole."

"Charming," Mike said.

"And here I was, trying to keep that a secret. Nice cap, by the way. Makes you look sophisticated."

She tilted her head. I could tell she just noticed my swollen jaw. "What happened to your face?"

"I was swapping out a component on one of the airport's runway towers when I slipped on some pigeon shit, fell, and landed on my jaw."

"You really need to quit lying so much," Mike said.

Jackie Frazier blinked. "Hurt much?"

"Only when I laugh."

"Good. Let me think up a good one."

"You shouldn't have taken her lighter," Mike said.

"You're still miffed about your lighter, aren'tcha?" I asked.

"Why am I here? I had a date for this afternoon. Two of my--uh, two old high school friends were supposed to pick me up. *You* wouldn't know anything about that, would you?"

"I really don't know what you're talking about."

She glared. "You think you're cute, but you're not. You're a moron."

"And you've never seen a cute moron before?"

"You don't qualify."

"Maybe if you'd worn a tie?" Mike said.

I ignored Mike. "If you're fishing for a date," I told the girl, "I'm busy tonight. Tomorrow's bad as well. Why don't you try me in a couple of weeks?"

"You'd have to hogtie me for that."

The image made my mouth water. "Now you're *really* turning me on. . ."

"You're sick. Are you gonna tell me why I'm here?"

"Everyone's got to be somewhere."

"Like I just said, you're not cute *at all*."

"Maybe your date had a prior engagement."

"You did this. I don't know how a jerk like you could, but you did *some*thing. What'd you do?"

"Actually, I've been in my apartment all afternoon, walking around in my shorts and flip-flops while contemplating the true meaning of plastic."

She glared at the big guy standing beside her. "This is *kidnapping*, you know. Unlawful imprisonment. I should call my father."

"That wouldn't be very bright. You don't want him learning about that bit of business you and your so-called high school friends have been doing lately. That new escort service in town? And don't forget what happened to Alan Smith and that loser, Pickett."

She blinked. "I don't know what you're talking about."

"By the way, that body-in-the-trunk thing was a nice touch. Not very convincing, though." She said nothing. "Was that your idea? Or one of your friends'?"

"I have no idea what you're going on about."

"Whatever. Ready to go?"

"You mean I can really *go*? With this *ape* standing here?"

"What about it, ape? What do you say?" He shrugged. "It's all right with him. Ready to go home now?"

She squinted. "Home?"

"Home. You know. There's no place like home? Click your heels together three times? The place where the heart is? That sort of thing?"

"I have other stuff to do, and you can just--"

"You haven't spent enough time with Mommy and Daddy. Apart from your dad's birthday party, you haven't been with them at all. Don't you think you'd better spend more time chatting with them about your latest ventures? Or maybe join them in a friendly game of canasta?"

"Listen, I've got plans for this afternoon, and they don't include my folks. Besides, my mother doesn't even expect to see much of me."

"Because?"

"I've got lots of friends. I'm really popular. Know how *that* is?" She snorted. "Sorry. That *was* rude, wasn't it?"

"You? Rude? How silly--and totally inaccurate."

"Who the fuck do you think you are?"

257

"Just an old, unpopular moron asked by a good friend to make sure you got safely off your plane."

"Your friend's an asshole, too. And if you think I'm gonna do what you say, you're full of shit."

"You can either do as I say, or you can do as they tell you at the Police Station. I prefer the Police Station. It's on the way back to my apartment anyway."

She stiffened. "I . . . haven't *done* anything!"

"I'll bet they can tie you in with the murders of Smith and Pickett--"

"You're full of shit. I don't even know who these people are!"

"That's beside the point. I think it would be interesting to see how deep a hole we can dig for you."

"Why are you *doing* this?"

"You're such a sweet kid."

"Listen." She squirmed in the chair, shifting her legs. "Maybe we can talk about this. Without *him* standing there."

"I was wondering when she'd try that," Mike said flatly.

"C'mon. Your ride leaves in five minutes."

"I'm not going anywhere until we talk this out."

I pulled out my cell phone. "A friend of mine at OPD is *real* interested in closing a couple of murder investigations."

She jumped up. "You can't *do* this to me!"

"Where's your luggage?"

She didn't reply. I went into the next room. There it was, standing on the floor at the foot of her bed--the damned thing that nearly popped my spine out of whack. Mr. Ape could take it from here. But before he took over, I had to satisfy my curiosity. I dropped it on its side and opened it. The pink glamour bells sat on top on her clothes.

She came in, fists clenched. "You can't *do* this! This is my stuff! My property! I'm gonna call my old man and--"

One of the dumbbells rolled off the pile and thumped quietly to the carpet. A tiny pink square of vinyl eased open from the round end. A small teaspoon of white powder trickled onto the rug.

The girl brought a hand up to her mouth.

"Oops," Mike said.

The bodyguard came in. His eyes lowered to the tiny mound on the floor.

"Whaddya think?" I asked him. "Talcum powder? Powdered milk? Or maybe something a tad stronger?"

He squatted, licked the tip of his index finger, and gently touched the powder. He applied it to his tongue. "High-quality."

The girl whimpered softly.

"I guess you can tell your boss we found the source."

He nodded.

"Smart way of getting it on a plane," I said.

He grabbed a ten-pounder, picked it up, shook it, and tossed it to me. I automatically grabbed it with both hands to prevent it from thumping my chest, then realized it weighed no more than a pound or two. "Hollowed out?"

He shrugged.

"They can't all be hollowed out."

"No need."

I picked up a three-pounder. It was just as heavy as the ten Raguzzo's man had tossed at me. "This one's legit."

At airport security, they'd probably just let them through the check-ins. Since the insides of the bells were probably made of poured concrete, the scanners wouldn't be able to penetrate. Using a drill, whoever did this could hollow it out, then pour the coke through a funnel.

"How much do you think?" I asked.

"You can prob'ly move a hundred K this way, easy." He straightened and pulled a cell phone out of his jacket pocket.

If they were all hollowed out, the suitcase wouldn't have been as heavy as it felt. But hollowing out just half the bells would keep the weight up, and still provide enough powder for a good score.

The girl's face was as white as a sheet as she stood in the doorway, shivering.

"Still want to call your old man?" I asked.

She covered her face with her hands and began to sob.

Chapter 21

That night, while Doc Severinsen and the Tonight Show Orchestra blasted through "*Begin the Beguine*" from my living room stereo, I fixed a strong drink.

My cell buzzed. It was Phil. "Why haven't you called me? I'd hoped you'd call around suppertime, but you didn't."

I didn't want to tell her what happened. And I certainly didn't want to tell her the trouble Jack Frazier's precious daughter was in. "Busy day," I said simply, then collapsed on the couch.

"Are you playing Doc Severinsen? Or that screechy Canadian guy?"

"Can't you tell the difference between Doc and Maynard Ferguson?"

"You know big band stuff isn't my thing."

"I've always managed to overlook your horrible taste in music."

"You think Bach is horrible? Mozart? Schubert? Stravinsky?"

"Too high-brow for my taste."

"I have no idea what you just said. The music is entirely *too loud*."

"Are you saying it's interfering with your thought processes?"

"I can't hear, either."

I got up and turned down the volume. "Better?"

"Much. So what happened?"

As I went back to the couch, I decided to tell Phil only what I considered necessary. "I found out a few things about a couple of really bad guys and got in touch with the right people to make sure these bad guys don't their thing in Orlando anymore."

"Do these bad people have anything to do with Jackie Frazier?"

"Let's just say they wanted to do some nasty stuff with her and leave it at that."

"*With* her? Or *to* her?"

She was asking too many questions. "Does it matter?"

"Not to us, but certainly to Jack and Ruth."

"Then we shouldn't worry about it, should we?"

"You're being your usual evasive self."

"Thank you."

"There must be a reason for it, I guess."

"You could be right."

"But not necessarily?"

"Maybe, maybe not."

A pause. "Are you saying Jackie's innocent of all this stuff going on?"

"Not exactly. . ."

"Then Jackie was *involved*?"

"Maybe, maybe not."

"Ralph, your evasiveness is really irritating."

"That's only because you're not leaving it at that."

"I guess I need to stop asking questions."

"Everything turned out all right and the bad guys are somewhere else."

"Where did they--"

"Phil."

"I guess I'll have to trust you on this."

"Try real hard."

She sighed. "I deserved that one."

"Yeah, you did."

"So . . . this brings us to the business part of this arrangement."

"You mean how much do you owe me?"

"Like I said, I'll pay you whatever you wish."

"All right. I used up about half a tank of gas. Give me twenty bucks and we'll call it even."

"Twenty *dollars*? For what *you* went through?"

"Too much?"

"What about all the aggravation you suffered?"

"You mean the unconscious thing? The kidnappings? Being forced to wear a hood against my will? The other unconscious thing? The swollen jaw? The body in my trunk? The trip to the Police Station?"

"What happened to your jaw?"

"How do you think I got unconscious the second time?"

"Is it . . . are you . . . your jaw isn't . . . are you all right?"

I loved to get her flustered. It told me the romance in our relationship hadn't died after all. "You still care, don'tcha?"

"Of course I care, silly. Were you hospitalized? Are you taking medication? I told you I'd pay you whatever--"

"I'm fine, Phil. Honest."

"But those nasty people. Those hoodlums. You need to be paid for all that."

"You really mean that?"

"Of course I do."

"All right. Thirty bucks should square us."

***

I decided to turn in early. It had been a couple of hectic days, and I was tired.

At a little after eleven, I slipped Clifford Brown into my CD player, turned it on soft, and sat down to take off my shoes. I pulled off my socks, stood up to pull down my pants, and stopped. Mike was leaning against the dresser in a red silk shirt, tan Capri's, and black leather pumps. "Don't stop on my account."

I was suddenly embarrassed but had no idea why. She'd probably been in this room many times before, without my knowledge, but I still had this crazy modesty thing keeping me from stripping further.

"Keep going," she said, an impish grin on her face. "You're on a roll. The sexy trumpet music's great for the occasion."

"You know, the more I see you, the more you sound like me."

"I don't know if that's good or bad. But please continue. It's been a while."

I didn't like the way she was looking at me. It made me wonder what she was up to. I sat back down on the bed. "That's all right."

She giggled. "Don't tell me you're *bashful*. . ."

"I just don't want to be frustrated. If I'm frustrated, I'll toss and turn all night and wake up a wreck."

"Why would you be frustrated?"

"Look at you. There's a mirror in the bathroom."

264

"I thought you liked what I wear."

How could females remain so dense even when they were dead? "I love what you wear."

"Then what's the problem?"

I shrugged. "You're dead."

"Oh. Sorry, I forgot."

"So why are you here?"

"I've found out a few things you might want to know."

"About what?"

"For one thing, the girl's having a really rough time. Her daddy brought in a staff of high-profile lawyers, but this is big, and the D.A.'s anxious to nail someone for all this. She knows she's going to have to tell them everything if she wants to stay out of prison."

"Good. She needs something like this to shock her into reality. Ever find out what happened with Alan Smith?"

"Not really, but apparently Paseo didn't lose any sleep over Smith's death. I figure Smith wanted to use his connection with Paseo to call the shots with the escort service and drug connection, but those two friends of his decided otherwise."

"I'll bet he threatened to bring in Paseo to scare them or bully them into letting him take over, so Armstrong and Dean paid Pickett do him in. I'll also bet Paseo's not his real name."

"It's Arturo Vega. He recently came up from Cuba, buying up real estate and setting up shop in Kissimmee. He moved in quickly to take over the protection rackets with the Hispanic-owned Kissimmee pawnshops and motels."

"Vega." The name twanged a nerve. "He wouldn't by any chance have a daughter, would he?"

"Martina. She's twenty-six, bright, multilingual, and does the books for her father."

"Smith probably decided to use her as a steppingstone when he joined Vega's organization. The fact that she's a hot-looking babe made it much easier."

"That's a good assumption."

"My ex owes me big-time for all this."

"She intends to pay you, right?"

"Damn right. She owes me thirty bucks for getting me involved in this mess."

Mike just looked at me.

"What can I say? I'm easy."

"And cheap."

"I prefer to say I'm more reasonable than my competitors."

"You still love her, don't you?"

Why were women so damned highly tuned to stuff like that? Even when they were dead, they still picked up on stuff that left men clueless. I just shrugged.

"I figured as much."

"You can't tell yourself who to love, you know."

"She still loves you, doesn't she?"

"I guess it's possible."

"She called you, didn't she?"

"She said she couldn't find anyone else."

Mike laughed. *"That's* what she told you?"

"Don't tell me you've become Dear Abby of the Afterlife?"

"That would be Flo's nickname. But I can still see the obvious."

"You and Flo sound really tight."

"She's sweet. She has this son who's a musician, and he always seems to get involved with the wrong people."

"That's one of the hazards of being a musician." I rubbed my eyes. "I'm really tired, Mike."

"Well, if you're not gonna continue undressing until I leave, I guess I should be leaving."

"Like I said, I'm tired. You wouldn't want me to try to sleep while I'm frustrated, would you?"

"Why, of course not, silly boy."

I got up and pulled down my pants. She'd already disappeared. I got into bed, turned off the lamp, and tried focusing on sleep. Maybe I'd get up early, drive to the office, and luck into a high-paying gig before lunch. If I decided not to go in, I'd put on Cat Anderson or Chet Baker, roll over, and go back to sleep.

When you own your own business, you can do whatever the hell you please.

THE END

OTHER BOOKS BY THE AUTHOR

THE APPRENTICE
WAGON DRIVER
DEMON CHASER
STEPPING OUT OF MY GRAVE
THE FUNNY DETECTIVE
WORKING FOR A MOB BOSS
LOOKING FOR A DEAD GUY
HUNTING THE TALL BLONDE
FAVOR FOR A FRIEND
DEMON CHASER II
ESCAPE CLAUSE
FATAL INNOCENCE
COLORS
AND DARKNESS FELL

Titles available through:
Fiction4All